Unbreak My Heart

Mimi

Lock Down Publications and Ca$h
Presents

Unbreak my Heart

A Novel by *Mimi*

Mimi

Lock Down Publications
Po Box 944
Stockbridge, Ga 30281

Visit our website @
www.lockdownpublications.com

Copyright 2022 by MiMi
Unbreak my Heart

First Edition August 2022
Printed in the United States of America

This is a work of fiction. Names, characters, places, and incidents either are products of the author's imagination or are used fictitiously. Any similarity to actual events or locales or persons, living or dead, is entirely coincidental.

Lock Down Publications
Like our page on Facebook: Lock Down Publications @
www.facebook.com/lockdownpublications.ldp
Book interior design by: **Shawn Walker**
Edited by: **Nuel Uyi**

Stay Connected with Us!

Text **LOCKDOWN** to 22828 to stay up-to-date with new releases, sneak peaks, contests and more...
Thank you.

Submission Guideline.

Submit the first three chapters of your completed manuscript to ldpsubmissions@gmail.com, subject line: Your book's title. The manuscript must be in a .doc file and sent as an attachment. Document should be in Times New Roman, double spaced and in size 12 font. Also, provide your synopsis and full contact information. If sending multiple submissions, they must each be in a separate email.

Have a story but no way to send it electronically? You can still submit to LDP/Ca$h Presents. Send in the first three chapters, written or typed, of your completed manuscript to:

LDP: Submissions Dept
Po Box 944
Stockbridge, Ga 30281

DO NOT send original manuscript. Must be a duplicate.

Provide your synopsis and a cover letter containing your full contact information.

Thanks for considering LDP and Ca$h Presents.

Dedication

For my father, Danny.
I love you to the stars and moon and back. Thank you for always having my back!

Mimi

Chapter One

Samara looked into the mirror at herself as she sang the hit song 'Not Gon' Cry' by Mary J. Blige. Samara wasn't much of a singer but when she did her one-woman performance, you couldn't tell her that she wasn't on stage in front of thousands of people. Samara picked up her flat iron and connected it to her hair, pulling it to create the bone-straight effect she was going for. She was dressed for the night, make-up was done, and all she had to do was complete her hair. It would help if she stopped thinking that she was performing.

For the night, Samara was dressed in a pink jumpsuit that had cut-outs from the underboob area that stopped just above her ankle. She was thankful that her mother passed her curves down to her. There would have been no way that she would have been able to pull this outfit off if she didn't have the body to match. On her feet were a pair of clear-pointed toe, six-inch stilettos. The finishing touches to her look were her diamond bangles, diamond necklace, and diamond stud earrings. If she had to say so herself, she looked damn good.

"I should've left your ass a thousand times!" Samara belted as if she was truly heartbroken and could carry a tune. When she was about to give the next line all that she had, the music stopped abruptly.

"Excuse you! My husband and I are trying to get some sleep!" the woman yelled. Samara turned around and looked at the culprit. Standing in front of her was her boyfriend's mother. Helen had been a pain in Samara's ass since the very first day she had met her.

"Well, maybe you and your husband need to find someplace else to live," Samara simply stated, turning her back to Helen, pressing the *play* button, and continued to do her hair. Helen walked over to the sink in the bathroom and pressed the power button on the Bluetooth speaker, cutting the music off yet again. Samara let her hair fall from the flat iron as she turned slowly to look at Helen. She looked at her in bewilderment as she shot daggers at Helen.

Mimi

"Excuse me. Just what the fuck you think you doing?" Samara questioned. Samara didn't care how she talked to Helen. In order to get respect, you had to give it and Helen never spoke to her that way, so she never did, until now. It didn't matter whether Helen was older than her or not.

"Who do you think you're talking to like that?" Helen asked, flabbergasted.

Samara knew what Helen was doing, and she refused to fall into the trap. Samara shook her head as she turned her body away from Helen and began to clean up her mess. She pressed the power button on the speaker and proceeded to ignore Helen. She had been dealing with this disrespect for two and a half years. She loved the shit out of Ryan but detested his mother. The music stopped again, and at that point Samara was ready to fight.

"Look, I'm going to tell you this one last time. Turn this nonsense off. My husband and I are trying to sleep!" Helen said with more authority in her tone.

Samara placed her hands on her hips and said: "Bitch, you got one more time to touch my shit. Try me and you're gonna be laying on this floor between the sink and the toilet."

"This is my son's house!"

"You see, that's what you think. My name is on the deed as well as his and if you want to keep trying me, you're gonna be on the street while I'm in here riding your son and your husband!"

Helen's eyes ballooned out of their sockets. None of Ryan's other girlfriends would ever talk to her like that and for that reason alone, she didn't like Samara. From the moment she met Samara, she knew she was no good for her son. To Helen, Samara was bottom of the barrel, gutter trash, never mind the fact that Helen herself was born and raised in the hood. She was raised on welfare, public assistance, and section 8 housing. Helen's mother, however, taught her daughter to never allow the way she grew up define her. To always be as classy and as regal as a queen was meant to be. When Helen left the hood, she vowed to never return or act as the many women she had seen in the ghetto. It took years, but if you didn't

10

know Helen you would think she grew up as a sheltered, suburban child.

"I don't know why my son chose you to be with. You are nothing but bottom-of-the-barrel scum. A true definition of a gutter rat!" Helen yelled.

"It amazes me that you look down at me like you weren't born and raised in the ghetto just like I was. You are so quick to judge me, but we are from the same damn hood. Just because you wear pantsuits and eat caviar and do nothing but spend your husband and son's money doesn't mean shit to me! I will never respect you for those things alone. Now keep touching my shit in my house and see if you won't get a beat down straight from a bitch who is proud to be from the hood!" Samara yelled. She was fuming. Usually she didn't let the shit Helen say get to her, but her utter disrespect towards Samara was building up and it would be a time where Samara was gonna explode like a bomb.

Ryan caught the end of what Samara was telling his mother as he walked into his home. This was the last thing that he wanted to have to deal with after a long evening of entertaining new clients. His girlfriend was the sweetest person he had known, and he also knew that she was vicious when provoked. He loved his mother, but he was getting tired of her verbal attacks on his girlfriend. Dropping his bag at the door, he ran upstairs to where the chaos ensued. Just as he reached the top, he saw his mother lunging at Samara and in just in the nick of time, his father grabbed his mother around the waist as she was in mid-swing. Samara stepped back to sidestep the hit but bounced right back on the balls of her feet, throwing a vicious right hook that landed on his mother's chin.

"Whoa! Whoa! Whoa! What the hell is going on?" Ryan asked as he held Samara's wrists and pushed his frame against hers, backing her into their bedroom.

"Paul, let me go! This ghetto wench hit me!" Helen yelled, trying to push her husband off of her.

"I'm tired of your ass talking crazy to me! And then you felt froggy enough to leap your crooked wig-wearing ass in my space. What the fuck you thought was going to happen?"

Mimi

"Dad, would you take mom back to y'all room!" Ryan pleaded with his father as his mother spilled venom towards Samara. Meanwhile, Paul struggled to move Helen. Samara raised her hands to her ears, placed her thumbs inside, and wagged them while sticking her tongue out in a taunting manner. If this wasn't his mother and girlfriend, Ryan would have laughed. Once Helen was out of view, Ryan closed the bedroom door and glared at Samara.

Scrunching up her face, Samara asked, "Why are you looking at me like that?"

"Did you have to hit her?" Ryan asked.

Samara walked inside of the bathroom to touch up her hair and make-up. She replied, "She stepped to me first. Are you kidding me? I would never swing on that old bitch first but you better believe that I don't have any problems beating her ass."

"Samara, would it hurt if you could be the bigger person?" Ryan asked. He loosened his tie as he sat in the high back chair that sat catty corner in the bedroom. Samara walked out of the bathroom, reapplying the gloss on her lips. For the first time since he's been home, he noticed the outfit she was wearing. Changing the subject, Ryan asked, "Where are you going dressed like that?"

"Sheeka asked me to go out with her tonight. Thanks to your bald headed ass mama, I'm late. I don't got no problem with Paul, but your mother gonna find herself beat the fuck up. When the fuck are they moving out?"

Helen and Paul's house caught fire one night, six months prior. They were going to a friend's house in their neighborhood for an event, and Helen had left her curling iron on. The curling iron was sitting on top of a dry rag, which eventually caught fire and everything went downhill after that. They left the party only to return home to everything they owned burned to a crisp and the fire department putting out the flames. That happened in January and now it was July, and his parents were still in their home. The arguments between Helen and Samara began as soon as Helen moved in. She tried to run their household as if it was hers. While Ryan didn't mind, Samara didn't like it one bit and she voiced her opinion every chance she got.

"Samara, we spoke about this. They are in the process of looking for one." Ryan sighed. He loved everything about Samara, but this ongoing situation was wearing thin on his nerves. Samara looked at Ryan sitting in the chair. He wore a denim blue Ferragamo suit, white button-up, blue tie, and black Ferragamo shoes. Even when he looked stressed, he was fine to Samara. She could see the heaviness that weighed heavy on his shoulders, and she wished that things were better. She wished that he stood up to his mother for her so she didn't have to do it and look like the bad guy. They barely argued before his parents moved in, and now it seemed like they argued three to four times a week. It was never Samara starting and Ryan knew this, but she always made it her business to finish it. Samara walked over to Ryan and squatted down in front of him, forcing him to look at her.

"Ryan, with everything in my body, I love you. I love you so much that I'm dealing with your disrespectful ass mama and keep giving her chance after chance. I don't give bitches in the street this many chances and your mama is wearing thin on my nerves. When she wasn't under the same roof, it was okay because I didn't have to deal with it that often. Ryan, baby, I can no longer deal with this type of disrespect and under my roof no less. Either they close on a house in the next three weeks or I'm gone until she's gone. I'll be back later on." Samara placed a kiss on Ryan's forehead before she stood and walked away. She didn't give Ryan ultimatums. He was such a man through and through and she never had to make him choose. The fighting was becoming too much for her to handle and she'd rather she gave him the ultimatum than give Helen the ass whooping she was begging for.

Samara was gone, and Ryan needed to know from his mother what happened. Samara was right. She was doing everything in her power to keep the peace, and his mother wasn't making it easy. Ryan stood from the chair and took his jacket off. Next was his shirt and pants. He needed a shower bad, and that's what he planned to do.

Ryan and Samara met at a subway. She was rushing out as he was coming in and when they collided, her food spilled all over the both of them. Even though it wasn't his fault, he immediately apologized and tried to help Samara clean herself off. He offered to buy her another meal and he was surprised that she accepted the offer. Samara had cursed him out like it had been his fault. He was being nice when he offered to pay for her meal. He could afford it but he was turned off by her attitude. When he ordered both of their meals, he decided to stay and eat inside of the restaurant. They connected and have been together since.

Ryan was ready to put a ring on Samara's finger, but before he did that he needed to get the issues with his mother under control. Ryan washed his body with lavender body wash to calm and relax his muscles, getting out when he felt his stress go down the drain with the water. Once he was dressed in basketball shorts and a beater, Ryan made his way downstairs to fix himself a drink. Ryan made himself a Tequila Sunrise, heavy on the Tequila, and walked into his living room to catch up on ESPN. Two hours passed before he knew it. His mind had been in overdrive thinking about what he should do with his home situation.

"Ryan?" Helen questioned. She had woken up thirsty and she was on her way to the kitchen when she noticed the light coming from the TV.

Ryan sat up on the couch, guzzling his fourth Tequila Sunrise. He responded: "Yes, ma."

"What are you doing up this late?" she asked, stepping through the living room threshold.

"Thinking, ma." Ryan sighed. He didn't know how to bring up what happened. He loved his mother and he didn't want to offend her, but he needed the chaos to stop. Ryan knew that Samara would keep her word and remove herself from the situation, and Ryan didn't want that.

Helen sat on the couch next to Ryan and asked, "What's on your mind, son?"

Ryan placed the glass he held onto the wooden coffee table in front of him. He sat back on the couch and looked at his mother. He asked, "Ma, what happened between you and Samara tonight? What I walked into was straight bullshit."

At the mere mention of Samara's name, Helen twisted up her face and grunted. If she knew this was what was going on in his head, she wouldn't have said anything. Huffing and puffing, Helen finally responded, "That tramp—"

Ryan interrupted, "She's my girlfriend. If you're gonna speak on her, use her name. Do not disrespect her."

Helen gasped in shock. Ryan had never spoken to her like that. For the sake of her son, she decided not to use words that disrespected Samara. Clearing her throat, she continued, "She was playing music way too loud and your father and I were trying to get some rest. All I did was ask her if she could low it down and she went all ghetto on me."

Ryan looked at his mother in disbelief. The lies fell from her lips so effortlessly. Ryan wasn't there and Samara didn't tell him what happened but he knew his girlfriend wasn't going to jump unless provoked.

"Ma, you can't sit there and lie in my face."

"Are you calling me a liar, boy?" Helen was furious. She stood up towering over Ryan's frame.

He looked up at her and replied, "I know Samara, ma. She's not gonna react unless she's provoked. What really happened?"

Helen folded her arms across her chest and huffed. She replied, "I don't know why you are with her. You know that she's only with you because of your money. You are literally making hundreds of thousands of dollars and it keeps going up because celebrities are now coming to you. That—that hussy is only with you for your money."

Ryan looked at his mother in disbelief. He knew that she wasn't serious. Ryan pinched the bridge of his nose and stood up from the couch. The cup he rested on the coffee table, he placed in his hand taking a hefty sip. Helen looked at her son's movements and knew that he was beyond pissed. Ryan had a very bad temper growing up and as an adult it sometimes reared its ugly head. Ryan moved to the door frame and leaned against the door frame of the living room.

"When I met Samara, she had a thriving boutique and she had come to me looking for a location for her second boutique. I wasn't nearly making what I make now, back then. Samara didn't give a fuck about my money. She was out getting that shit way before I came into the picture. But you wouldn't know that now, would you? From the day you met her, you decided to judge her because she wants my money."

Helen stood with her arms folded as she listened to her son. She knew he was right. She never gave that girl a chance. And as long as she was breathing, she would never give her the chance. Helen walked up to Ryan and bore her eyes into his. She said, "A mother knows when someone is for their child. Yes, I went and said something to her about her music and yes, it was nasty. I make no apologies. She is no good for you and I will never get along with that tramp."

"You are not going to continue to disrespect her in her house," Ryan calmly stated and walked away to the kitchen. Helen followed him.

"I am your mother, Ryan. I don't care whose house it is. If I'm in it then I should be respected."

"Well then, ma, you leave me no choice to help assist you and dad in finding a house. I love Samara and plan to marry her one day. If you don't like it, you don't have to support it. That simple. But the disrespect to Samara stops today. Do you understand?" Ryan spoke sternly. He was trying his hardest not to disrespect his mother. So with that statement, he placed his cup in the sink and went up to his bedroom to go to bed. It was only one in the morning and he knew that when Samara was done partying with her friends, she would be staying at her sister's house. She always did when she had gotten into it with his mother. That was going to come to a stop because come hell or high water, his parents were getting out of his house fast.

Chapter Two

Samara woke up at her sister's house after a night of partying. She was on the long couch while her friend—Sheeka—was on the love seat. The fullness from her bladder was what had awakened her from her slumber. She walked down the long hallway to the bathroom to relieve herself. Her breath was tart, and the taste of last night's alcohol lingered on her breath. When she was done emptying her bladder, she washed her hands, reached under the bathroom sink for the extra toothbrush that she knew her sister had, and proceeded to make sure her mouth was clean. Exiting the bathroom, she passed by her sister's room and heard her voice. She knocked before she opened the door and saw Samirah on the phone. Samirah waved her in and ended the phone call.

"You sober, bitch?" Samirah asked with a cackle as she sat up in bed.

"As sober as I can be right now. What time is it?"

"Almost eleven. I don't even know how you are up right now."

"Shit, your guess is as good as mine. I got to get ready to leave. I got to open up the shop today at one."

"Before you go, I need you to tell me what happened now between you and the wicked witch from the west."

"How do you know something happened?" Samara asked, looking at her sister. Of course Samirah knew something happened; they were sisters and knew each other like the back of their hands.

Samirah looked at Samara like she had two heads. She replied, "I know you better than you know yourself. If you must know, when that evil witch does something to disturb you, you come here. So spill it, what she do?"

Samara thought about what happened the previous night. Even though she was out having fun, she still pondered about the whole situation and felt slightly guilty about her actions. Yes, she was being provoked but the situation could have been avoided if she would have just walked away. There was just something about it that ate at her every time Helen had something to say to her. With a heavy sigh, she told her sister what happened.

"Bitch, when she swung at me, all I wanted to do was drag that hoe through the house," Samara said after running the story down to Samirah.

"You should have. That old bitch got some damn nerve."

"Sis, I don't know what to do. I love Ryan with everything in me but I can't continue to deal with the disrespect. I would have broken that bitch face but Ryan kept saving her. Oh, and let's not forget the fact that he never believes me when I tell him it's his bald headed hoe ass mama that is starting. I don't want to leave him because that shit seems like a petty ass reason to leave him."

Samirah sat up and looked at her sister seriously. She said, "Then don't allow the old bitch to win. Put your foot down, Samara. I've never known you to allow this type of shit to happen. You are a strong person. Go home and talk with Ryan. If nothing changes then you know what you have to do."

Samara thought about what Samirah said. Reaching over, she wrapped her arms around her sister and thanked her. Samara left the room, waking Sheeka up before going on the Lyft app and placed a request for a driver. Sheeka was dropped off first, giving Samara time to gather her thoughts. She hated having to stoop down to give Ryan an ultimatum, but she believed that if their love was as strong as she thought, Ryan would do anything to make sure that he kept her around. She got so lost in her thoughts, she didn't realize that she had arrived home. She thanked the driver and exited the car.

Samara looked up at the house that she called home for the past year. With a heavy sigh, she walked to the door in her bare feet. There was no way she was putting shoes on after a night of dancing. The house was quiet when she entered, which would have made sense being that there were no children in the house.

"Ryan!" Samara called out. She walked around the first level of the home and didn't see Ryan. She made her way upstairs into their bedroom. He wasn't there either, and she knew he could be in one other place. It was Saturday. He wasn't working, so she knew he would be in the backyard, sitting on the swing under the gazebo. Samara turned around to walk out of the bedroom. Paul's presence startled her.

"Oh shit! Paul, you scared the shit out of me," Samara said, holding her hand to her chest as if she was having a heart attack.

Paul chuckled and replied, "I'm sorry. I didn't mean to. I heard you calling for Ryan and decided to take this moment to apologize for Helen's actions."

"Paul, you don't have to apologize. You did nothing wrong. Helen needs to apologize but we both know that she won't. I appreciate you for doing so but that is not for you to do." Samara felt bad for Paul. He was a man through and through, but around his wife, he clams up like a bitch and allows her to dictate everything.

"I do have to apologize. She won't and it is owed to you. Ryan is in the backyard," Paul replied and walked away. Samara dropped her shoes off in her bedroom and made her way down to the backyard. Still in her outfit from last night, Samara sashayed her way to the gazebo with a smile on her face. Ryan looked up from the work that he was doing, and looked up at Samara with a smile of his own.

"By the way, your lashes are hanging on. I can tell you had a good night!" Ryan joked, bringing laughter from Samara. He removed the laptop from his lap, opening his arms for Samara to sit on his lap and melt into him.

"When I'm dancing, I'm always having a good time," Samara said, placing her face into his neck. Ryan always smelled good. Today she knew that he had showered and moisturized his skin with *Sauvage* by Dior. Her favorite scent on him. They sat there momentarily in silence. Samara listened to the thud of his heart. A rhythm she could listen to forever.

"Babe, I need to talk to you," Ryan spoke. He tapped her arm to signal that it was serious and he needed her to look at him. Samara sat up, folding her legs up under her body, and placed her hair in a messy bun. Ryan looked at Samara, taking in her features. She had a resemblance to Ryan Destiny. Ryan smiled as his heart thundered in his chest. He wasn't nervous. He was in love with this woman and vowed to do everything in his power to make her happy.

"Things around here have been a little chaotic lately and it seems like it's putting a strain on our relationship. Last night was the last straw when I walked in. I don't know how much you have endured for the past few months and I apologize for not listening to you and ignoring you. I can tell you're not happy and my intentions were to never make you feel that way. I should have listened to you when my parents first came to stay."

Samara interrupted and asked, "What? That you should have helped them find a house instead of letting somebody at the office do it for you? Hmm?"

Ryan smirked and replied: "Yeah, that. I should have listened, babe, and I'm sorry. I'm helping them now and I'm taking them to go see one today. Before I go though, I need to show you something."

Ryan gathered up his things and had Samara follow him into the house. He placed his things on the kitchen counter and then made his way into the living room. Helen was in there, placing her earrings in her ears.

"Hmm. The cat done brought a whore home!" Helen spat with disgust.

Samara chuckled and was about to respond but Ryan spoke up. He said, "Ma, didn't I just tell you last night that you are not to disrespect Samara in her house. And whatever you just said didn't make any sense."

"If you heard her tell me what she said to me last night, you would think the same thing too."

Samara rolled her eyes and chuckled. Ryan looked at Samara with a questioning look and she proceeded to explain. She said, "She tried me and I told her if she kept trying me that I would be in here riding both you and Paul."

Helen tooted her lips as both Ryan and Samara howled in laughter. Wiping the tears from the corners of his eyes, he turned towards Samara with a seriousness on his face. He said, "I know that you have to go open the shop but there is something that I need to say. Before I met you, I thought finding love was useless. After my last girlfriend took my heart and broke it into tiny pieces, I lost hope. But baby, you made me believe in love again. I don't know what you did but I am in love with you, Samara. I said all of that to say this: I want to be with you forever, Samara. Grow old with you, raise our kids together. Would you do the honor of becoming my wife?"

Both Helen and Samara gasped as Ryan bent down on one knee and produced a black velvet ring box. Inside was a two and half carat pear-shaped diamond ring. Round diamonds lined the frame, and the band was set in platinum.

Helen jumped up from the couch and pushed against Ryan's arm. She yelled, "No! No! No! You will not marry this whore! I won't allow it."

"Dad! Come get your wife! I'm trying to make Samara mine!" Ryan yelled, trying to stop Helen from pushing him over. Paul came rushing down the stairs and pulled his wife away from their son.

"What do you say? I know this is probably not what you thought how you would get engaged, but no setting could ever determine my love for you. So?"

Samara looked at Helen dead in the eyes as she said, "Hell yeah."

Ryan placed the ring on Samara's finger as the color drained from Helen's face. Ryan took Samara into his arms. He was the happiest man in the world at that moment, and not even his mother's sour mood could extinguish that. Paul congratulated both Ryan and Samara before he left the room once the ring was placed onto Samara's finger.

Ryan smiled at Samara. "I'm going to let you go because you have shit to take care of, but tonight we celebrate. That's what I was taking care of when you walked outside. Everything will be laid out for you when you get home." Ryan placed a kiss on her forehead. With a smile on her face she left the room and went to get ready to open her store.

7:00 P.M.

It was finally closing time and Samara couldn't be happier. As soon as the boutique was closed, Samara came out of her office to help the two women fix the store. She was cool with both Terri and Amber, but Amber had a special place in Samara's heart. Samara only had the boutique open for nine months when she met Amber. She was about to close the store when a very scared Amber ran through the door.

"Woah! Woah! Are you okay?" Samara asked. She began to walk towards Amber whose eyes were wide open.

"Please tell me you have a lock on the door! Please lock the door!" Amber yelled. Without question Samara ran over to the door and locked it shut while pulling the shades down over the windows. When she finished, Samara pulled Amber into her office and closed the door. Amber immediately fell to the floor into a heap. She cried hard. Samara didn't know what to do, but with one look at Amber she knew something was terribly wrong. Amber was dressed in blue distressed jeans, a white ripped V-neck short-sleeved top, and Vans. There were stains of dirt and dried blood on both her jeans and shirt. Amber's caramel-colored skin was black and blue on the exposed parts. Samara dropped down and wrapped her arms around Amber in comfort. They must have sat on the floor for an hour before Samara got Amber off of the floor and onto the couch to sip on some chamomile tea.

"I need to know your name and what happened tonight," Samara stated while she sipped on her own cup of tea.

Amber sighed. She was scared to tell anyone what had happened. She didn't want to bring anyone else in on her mess. She looked at Samara, and everything about her screamed trustworthy. She didn't look down at her with judgment like so many people have. Her eyes were soft and welcoming, and that's what she needed at that current time.

"My name is Amber. My boyfriend abused me. The first time he did it, he said that it wouldn't happen again. My mama always told me that if a man puts his hands on you, he doesn't love you and if he promises not to do it again, he will. I knew it was a red flag but I stayed. I stayed because I loved him. I loved him so much that I stopped loving myself in the process." Amber sniffled as the tears streamed down her face. She continued, "He went months almost a year without putting his hands on me. Then one day he had gotten

22

into an accident and when he got home, he blamed me. I didn't notice that there was something wrong with me. He got wild incessantly over every little thing."

"Oh my God! Amber. I am so sorry this has happened to you." Samara sympathized while rubbing Amber's back.

"I tried leaving. I even went to his church where his mother went. All of the married women there told me that he was just being a man. The single women looked at me with angry glares for me bringing my drama there. Nobody had compassion."

"What happened tonight? Obviously something happened because hun, it's like ten degrees outside and you don't have a coat on."

Amber looked up at the ceiling, trying to stop the tears that were threatening to spill from her eyes. She concentrated on her breathing by taking deep breaths through her nose and then exhaling out of her mouth. Several minutes passed by before Amber said, "I went to the store for groceries and when I got back, he was in bed with another man. He was taking this man's dick in his ass. The man jumped off of him, grabbed his clothes and left. I tried to kill Raymond but he was too big for me. He beat my ass until I faked like I lost consciousness. He left me alone. He panicked because he thought I died when I stopped moving. As soon as he saw my chest rising and falling, he walked away. I laid there for ten minutes thinking he had gone into the room. I was sadly mistaken when I made a bee-line for the back door, whereas he was leaning against the counter as I swung the door open and bolted through the night air. I jumped over gates and fell into mud, wet snow, and dirt. He almost got me until police sirens slowed him down. I ran down the alley two blocks over. Your store lights are what saved me."

Samara couldn't believe what she had just heard. She didn't know what to say, so she just rubbed Amber's back. The buzzer to her shop went off and soon after there was knocking. Amber and Samara looked at each other. Samara jumped up from the couch and went behind her desk to grab her rose gold .380 Ruger pistol.

"Please don't go out there. He's going to hurt you." Amber cried into the palms of her hands.

Mimi

Holding her right hand, with the gun, Samara said, "I wish the fuck he would. Stay right here. I promise you he won't get over the threshold."

Samara left her office and made it to the front of the shop. As she made her way to the door, she cursed herself for leaving the lights on. As soon as she turned the locks, the knocking stopped.

"Can I help you?" Samara asked. The man that stood in front of her was huge. He had to be at least six foot five inches compared to Amber's five foot four inches. From the looks of it, he looked to weigh damn near close to three hundred pounds.

"Sorry to bother you, but I noticed your lights on and wondered if you saw my girlfriend. We had a terrible argument and she walked away." Raymond explained, trying to appear as if he was sad. Samara wanted to laugh right in his face, but instead decided to keep her composure.

"No. My shop is closed and I haven't seen a single person in almost an hour." Samara lied with a straight face. Her gun was in her left hand and her trigger finger was eager for him to bust a move. Samara was ambidextrous and her left hand aim was just as on point as her right. Samara watched him as his eyes moved over top of her head, quickly scanning the store.

"Ma'am, are you sure? I would hate for you to be dragged into something that doesn't have anything to do with you!" Raymond threatened.

Samara rolled her eyes and replied: "Yeah, sure. Have a good night."

Samara moved to close the door as Raymond turned to walk away. The door was almost closed when Raymond pushed the door, causing Samara to fly across the room, gun still in hand. When she landed with a thud to the ground, the gun slid from her fingers and under a nearby clothes rack. Raymond walked over the threshold with a menacing glare. His eyes swept across the room, looking for Amber. Samara winced as she got up and slowly moved her way to the gun.

"Why did you lie to me? I know she is here. I just want my girl and we will be on our way." Raymond taunted, walking toward the

24

counter where the register was. That worked in Samara's favor because his eye wasn't on her. She was getting close to the gun when Raymond swung around in her direction. Samara paused and sat straight up, glaring at Raymond.

"Whoever you are looking for ain't here. You already knocked me down. I would appreciate it if you left before the police got here!" Samara stated as she got off of the floor where she inched closer to the clothing rack. Samara thanked God that the gun landed under the dress rack. The bottoms of the dresses concealed the gun perfectly.

"Amber!" Raymond yelled. He noticed the doorway behind the register and smirked. He had turned his back on Samara, and she dodged under the dress and retrieved the gun, instantly putting a bullet in the chamber. The sound instantly caused Raymond to pause in his footsteps.

"I said go before the police get here," Samara stated, hands wrapped tightly around the handle of the gun.

With a smirk on his face, Raymond started walking towards Samara. He paused when he got to the counter. He said, "You want to put that down? I only want Amber and I will be out of your way. No fuse, no muse."

"Stay the fuck right there and don't move," Samara said sternly. As she looked at Raymond, amusement danced in his eyes. The moment he lifted his foot and placed it down walking towards Samara, she squeezed the trigger, sending a bullet into his knee. Raymond instantly dropped to the floor, screaming like a little bitch. With the gun aimed at Raymond, Samara walked up on him.

"Let me make this shit clear. A woman beater is something I don't like. You 'bout to go to jail and I don't know how long you're gonna have but when you leave this store in them cuffs, Amber never existed to you. You will not contact her while you are in prison or whenever you get out. If she tells me—no, if she even utters your name, I promise you I won't aim for your knee!" Samara stated. There was a crazy look in her eye that Raymond didn't want to test. He let his head hit the ground in defeat. Samara called Amber from the back so she could call the police. Amber did what she needed to do and their friendship had solidified since then.

***

"Girl, I can't believe that Ryan popped the question." Amber swooned over Samara's hand with the engagement ring. They had been closed for half an hour and were getting ready to leave.

"I know. I'm still in shock that he did. It was worth the color draining from his mother's face." Samara laughed as she remembered Helen's face in her mind.

Amber rolled her eyes and replied, "That old hag needs to get over herself. She in Ryan business like she the one fucking him. When is she moving out?"

"Ryan says he's going to be helping his parents find a house and if you ask me, he should have done that from the jump. But I get that he wanted them to have that control, but shit—his mother is draining."

Ding!

The sound of Samara's phone going off put a pause on their conversation. Samara grabbed it from the counter and noticed that she had a message request on Facebook Messenger. Opening the notification, her face scrunched up due to her not recognizing the profile picture. This was her personal page, and she wondered who it was.

"What the fuck?" Samara said when the message opened.

Amber raised an eyebrow and asked, "What happened?"

The anger on Samara's face was pretty evident. Amber didn't know what it was that changed her friend's attitude but whatever it was, she knew it wasn't good.

"Look at this shit," Samara said as her phone clinked onto the counter. Amber peered over and her mouth dropped at what she saw.

"Who is that?" Amber asked.

Samara picked up the phone and re-read the message. There was a female in her inbox asking her if she knew who Ryan was.

Samara was getting ready to respond when another message came through. Samara went from mad to heartbroken in a matter of seconds. The second she decided that she wasn't going to respond, another message popped up.

Raegan Lee: I see you saw my message so I'm guessing I got the right person. Just so you know, me and Ryan have been fucking with each other off and on and have a child on the way. He's not gonna leave his family so you might as well run along and sink your claws into somebody else's man.

This infuriated Samara, and she felt her blood boiling. Samara wasn't the one to be a keyboard gangsta but this Raegan person real deal had her and Ryan fucked up. Samara had no doubt that Ryan wasn't doing what this woman claimed he was. Samara replied to the woman, telling her to get her goofy ass out of her inbox, and then she blocked the woman. Samara didn't have time to play with this lady and her shenanigans. However, Samara was going to make sure Ryan heard about this when she got home.

"Girl, don't let that shit bother you. She's probably delusional and can't let Ryan go. You just got engaged to the love of your life and y'all celebrate that tonight. Go home, live it up, and fuck what that lady saying." Amber headed to the door. She looked back at Samara and said, "I will see you at the party. Go talk to Ryan and after that, y'all just move on from that dumb shit."

"You're right. I'll see you there," Samara stated with a half smile on her face. Amber walked out of the store, locking the door behind her. Ten minutes later, Samara was leaving and heading home. On the drive home, she tried to listen to Jazz on her way home to get her mind off of Raegan and the messages, but her gut was telling her that it was deeper than the delusional woman. Something wasn't sitting quite right with her and after the party she was going to find out what was exactly going on.

When Samara walked into her home, there were a slew of people running around to get things in place. A blur of black and white outfits whipped around her. The kitchen, deck, and backyard was decorated in bright light, balloons, and tons of flowers. There were two long tables that sat at least twenty people apiece. Samara noticed the intimacy of it all, but she was on the prowl to find the man that she is going to be married to. Samara turned her attention to their bedroom. To get to their bedroom, Samara had to pass by Paul and Helen's room. She heard Helen talking, and she just knew that Helen was on the phone because she saw Paul in the backyard telling the crew where to set things up. Samara grabbed the door handle and quietly twisted it to open the door.

"What do you need two-hundred dollars for?" Helen asked. Her uppity voice was gone and the hood one was in full effect. Samara was going to leave but hearing what Helen had to say next put pause in her step and she stayed to continue to listen. Helen continued, "What are you going to do for this two-hundred dollars?" And then Helen paused to listen to the person on the other line. Helen's loud cackle made Samara jump in her skin and then Helen said, "You really think you got two-hundred dollars' worth of dick? I'm surprised that you think that. Now that head on your shoulders is worth it. I have an event to attend with my son tonight but when I'm done I'm going to call you."

Samara couldn't believe her ears as she filled with disgust. Paul was a good man. A little on the meek side but either way, he didn't deserve what Helen was doing. An idea clicked in Samara's head as she flung open with a smirk on her face. Helen's eyes popped out of her head as she quickly hung up the phone.

"What are you doing here? Don't you know how to knock?" Helen's uppity voice returned as she glared at Samara.

"Well, well, well. What was that I just heard you giving somebody two hundred dollars for some head? Does Paul know that his wife is out here tricking for niggas to give her head?" Samara spoke with ice in her tone and her face set in a scowl.

"You don't know what you heard, but I can assure you that it wasn't what you just said."

"You're not only a bully but you are also a liar and a whore. I wonder what Paul would say about this. I bet it would break his heart and he would divorce you and leave your gutter ass with nothing. And the best part about it, I will make sure personally that he does just that."

The look of terror that graced Helen's face caused Samara to chuckle sinisterly. Samara turned to leave and just as one of Samara's feet touched the hallway, Helen yelled, "Wait!"

Pausing in her footsteps, Samara placed a closed lip smile on her face and turned towards Helen. Samara asked, "What?"

"What do you want?" Helen asked with her lips pinned tight together.

"What do you mean what do I want?"

"What do you want from me in order to keep your mouth shut about this?"

Samara now understood what Helen was implying. Her mind started to spin as she thought about what she really wanted. Helen probably was thinking along the lines of money, but Samara's mind began to spin at the endless possibilities. Samara said, "I want you to accept the first house that Ryan finds for you and Paul. I don't care if it doesn't have everything you want in it. I don't care if it's ugly. You will take your old ass out of Ryan and I's relationship. Whenever you see me, you will respect me and in turn I will do the same."

As much as Helen wanted to tell Samara where to go, she knew she was in no position to do so. She would be ruining her marriage even more when it comes to Samara telling Paul what she heard. Helen stood up and looked directly at Samara and said, "Fine."

"You got one time to disrespect me and Paul will know immediately."

With a nod of Helen's head, Samara bounced out of the bedroom with her attention now on Ryan. She had a bone to pick with him as well. Ryan was in the bathroom brushing his teeth. A smile spread on his face when he spotted Samara behind him in the mirror.

"Hey, wife to be," Ryan said as he faced Samara and wrapped his arms around her. She gave him a one-arm hug, and maintained her resting bitch face.

"What's up?" she asked with a no-nonsense tone.

Ryan caught on to her tone and immediately rinsed the toothpaste from his mouth. He faced her and said, "You good?"

"Nah. Who is Raegan?"

"Raegan? She was my ex before I met you. Why?"

"I got an interesting message from her claiming that y'all are still together and she's pregnant with your baby."

Ryan's right eye twitched as he asked, "What? That's not possible because I haven't spoken to her in years. I knew this was going to happen."

Samara raised her brow and asked, "What do you mean you knew this was going to happen?"

Ryan leaned against the sink. He ran his hand down his face, debating whether or not he should get into this now. The look on Samara's face explained it all. He knew they weren't leaving the bathroom until he explained the situation to her.

"I dated her maybe twelve years before I met you. After I broke up with her, we went our separate ways until she found out I was in a relationship. She did the same exact thing. Just block her and I will figure out a way to handle this. Right now, can we just enjoy our night. This party was on such short notice and I don't want to ruin it by being late."

Samara looked at Ryan to see if she could detect any lies from him. She didn't, so she left it alone. Planting a kiss on his lips, she proceeded to undress and shower. Samara was satisfied with Ryan's response in the meantime. She would believe otherwise when he started to show her something else. Until then, she was going to slay in her evening gown with her fine ass fiancé and enjoy the night.

Chapter Three

A Year and Three Months Later

Samara looked at herself in her full-length mirror and a smile spread across her face. Today would be the day that she would officially become Mrs. Mumford. Since Samara had caught Helen tricking, Helen had been on her best behavior. Ryan and Paul were clueless as to why Helen changed her attitude toward Samara. Luckily for Helen, the first house her son showed her, she fell in love with it. After Samara confronted Ryan about Raegan, by the end of the night she forgot all about her and the messages that she had sent.

Samara's dress was royal blue. She didn't want the traditional white because nothing about her was traditional. It was haltered with Swarovski crystals along the breast and down her stomach, as if they were a waterfall. The dress showed off her curves just enough to still deem the dress as classy. The train of her dress wasn't that long, maybe extending five feet behind her. Her hair was slicked back into a ponytail that hung all the way down to her ass, and she opted for a tiara instead of a veil. As she looked at herself in the mirror, there was a knock on the door and in walked Samirah.

"Oh my God! You look beautiful, sis!" Samirah gasped as she came inside the room. Samirah was holding Samara's bouquet. They were royal blue and white roses, framed in Queen Anne's Lace. The stems were wounded tightly together with royal blue and white sashes.

"Thank you. You are too. I'm just mad it took me getting married in order for you to put on a dress." Samara shaded, causing both of them to laugh. Samirah was Samara's maid of honor and her yellow dress was slightly different from the yellow dresses her bridesmaids, Sheeka and Amber, were wearing.

"Get all of the pictures that you can because me and dresses don't mix." Samirah hated wearing dresses because she felt like she was too skinny and dresses made it look like a sheet was draped across her body.

"I'm gonna get your ass in a dress, sooner than you think. Is everyone here?"

"Yes, that's why I am here. To bring you your flowers and to come get you. Everybody is waiting on you."

Samara took one last look at herself in the mirror before she grabbed her bouquet. With a nod and a slight smile on her face, they walked out of the hotel room. Ryan and Samara decided on having their wedding at The Glen Sanders Mansion located in Scotia. There were several areas of the mansion that were perfect for pictures, especially with the view of the Mohawk River as the backdrop.

Samara stopped walking just before the door she was set to walk out of. She was watching Sheeka's back as she walked down the aisle with one of Ryan's groomsmen. When they were in place, John Legend's *Stay With You* started to blare through the speakers. Everyone stood up as Samara began walking down the aisle. The gasps from people made Samara nervous as she focused her attention on Ryan. He stood there fine as hell in a white Armani tux, a royal blue button up, with royal blue alligator skin shoes on his feet. Ryan's eyes misted over as he tried to hold his shit together, watching the love of his life walking towards him. After what seemed like an eternity, Samara finally reached Ryan. She held her tears back as hard as she could, but once she was in Ryan's face and noticed that he'd been crying, she broke down.

Ryan placed a gentle kiss on her nose and said, "You look so fucking beautiful."

Samara whispered into Ryan's ear, "You look pretty scrumptious yourself."

John Legend stopped playing as the pastor from Helen's church approached the couple and stood behind the microphone. He began: "Good afternoon, everyone. Today, we are gathered here to witness the union of Samara Porter and Ryan Mumford. Before we get into exchanging vows, I would like to pose the question to everyone here. If there is anyone here who has an objection to this union, please speak now or forever hold your peace."

Immediately, Samara glared at Helen, daring her to say something. Helen bowed her head into her lap and didn't utter a word.

The pastor waited a few seconds and when nobody said anything, he opened his mouth to begin but was stopped prematurely when the sound of clapping came from where Samara just exited from. Coming down the aisle were three women dressed in shorts, boots, tank tops, and scarves on their hands. Samara looked from the women to Ryan and saw the color drain from his face. Everyone looked on in confusion. Samirah, Sheeka, and Amber had already slipped their heels off just in case something popped off. Samara immediately recognized the barefaced beauty in front of her. She tried to let her hands go from Ryan's hands but he held them tight. However, she kicked her heels off as soon as she realized he wasn't going to let her hands go.

"I got an objection," the ring leader stated.

"Raegan, what are you doing here?" Ryan seethed through his teeth.

"I told you, over my dead body will you marry this bitch. You told me to give you time to tell her but here you are about to marry her. And the fucked up thing about it, Ryan—I had to hear this shit from my mama as I was dropping your son off!" Raegan yelled. Samara's stomach knotted as she remembered the message that Raegan had sent her over a year ago. The crowd was quiet as they watched in confusion.

"Ryan, you told me that she was obsessed with you and that would handle it. Why is she here on my wedding day implying that you were supposed to tell me something and she had your baby?" Samara asked with a scary calming tone.

"Baby I can—"

"Bitch, I'm not implying shit! All those business trips he said he was going on, you believed him, and he was right at my house. I warned you over a year ago and you didn't take heed. Now I'm here to get my nigga back so that we could go home and raise our baby." Raegan smirked.

Samara looked at Ryan. She trusted this man. She loved this man with everything in her body, so much so, before Raegan came in with her shenanigans, she was about to change her last name. Samara would have given up everything just to be with Ryan.

33

"Samara, I love you. I made a mistake and I'm willing to do anything to make this right." There was panic in his tone. Everything in Samara wanted to believe him, but he did the unthinkable. How would she ever trust him again? Within two seconds, Samara snatched her hands from Ryan's and was jumping from the platform she was standing on and landed on top of Raegan. Sheeka, Amber, and Samirah followed behind and jumped on Raegan's two friends. The venue was in utter chaos as Samara pummeled Raegan in the face. Ryan grabbed Samara off of Reagan when he saw blood. Paul and Ryan's groomsmen were able to pull the bridal parties off of the other women. However, it was too late. The police showed up.

"Ryan, how dare you! I asked you a year ago who this bitch was and you downplayed it like she was some crazy stalker! I gave you the opportunity for you to come clean and keep this shit a buck with me! And you lied to my face! Get your bitch up off the floor and get the fuck from my life!" Samara yelled, prepared to walk away. That was until she heard Raegan's voice.

"She was the one who put her hands on me! I'm pressing charges and I want her arrested!" Raegan yelled.

Samara was speechless. She was silent as the cops placed her wrists in cuffs and began to lead her to the car. As she walked past Raegan, she flared at her and said, "It would take a scary ass bitch to come cause chaos and then when you get your ass handed to you, you want to play victim. Let me tell you this though, sis. I don't give a fuck about jail and I damn sure don't care about that restraining order that you're about to have against me. Just know I'm coming for you. You thought that ass whopping was something? You just watch, bitch."

"Okay, that's enough! Let's go!" said the officer who had cuffed Samara.

"Baby, I'm right behind you to bail you out!" Ryan shouted as Samara was placed in the back seat of a squad car staring straight ahead.

"No, you don't. You are going to go pick up your son from my mama house so I can go to the hospital!" Raegan yelled.

"Raegan, we are still waiting for the DNA test to get back, so I don't even know why you came up here with all that bullshit. I told you already that I'm not doing shit until the results come back. You better miss me with that bullshit."

One of Raegan's friends came up behind her and pulled on her arm to get her to walk away. She spoke, "Raegan, I told you coming here was going to be a waste of time. I told you this was how this was going to turn out. He still a fuck nigga like he was back in the day."

Ryan looked on. He knew Tashia better than Raegan thought he knew her. His jaw twitched as he ran his thumb across his nose before he made the decision to belt out, "I'm such a fuck nigga, Tashia, but remember back in the day when me and Raegan was kicking it tough, you was swinging off my nuts just like she was. Remember when we went to that Jodeci concert and Raegan got drunk? We put her in the back seat of my car and you sucked my dick on the ride back? Huh? You don't remember that? What about the time she went back home to Atlanta to go bury her grandmother and you let me fuck you the whole two weeks she was gone? Do you remember that?"

"Ryan!" Paul called sternly enough to get his son's attention. Raegan's mouth was gaped open as she listened with torture to the man of her life, the father of her child, and the only man on earth that she has ever loved. She listened intently as he admitted to fucking her best friend while she was at her lowest.

The little bit of people that still lingered around gasped at what Ryan disclosed. Tashia looked as if she wanted to die right then and there. She was fucked up for days behind what she did, and wanted to take that secret with her to the grave, no matter how wrong she was. What she wasn't counting on was Ryan bringing that shit up. Tashia looked at Raegan and with speed like lightning, Raegan was hawling off, cocking Tashia dead in the eye.

"Bitch, you called yourself my friend! You told me to let this nigga go, all for what? For you to go behind my back and fuck the one nigga you knew that I loved with everything in my damn body!" Raegan yelled. Tashia stood off to the side with her hand up to her eye. She knew she was wrong which was why she didn't bother to fight back.

"I'm over this shit. I'm going to go get my girl back!" Ryan said with a wave of his hand, dismissing the situation. Ryan's best friend walked alongside him, telling him how bad he fucked up while asking Ryan was there anything he could do, all in the same breath. Several guests, along with Paul and Helen, helped the staff of the mansion clean up the mess before everyone called it a day.

The Next Morning

Samara woke up with aches and pains all over her body. She was cold and her head banged. She had never been to jail, and she was making sure that she wouldn't be having an extended stay. Samara wanted nothing more than to make sure that her sister and friends were good. She never suspected that they would be carted off to jail as well. If she would have known that Raegan was a scary bitch, she wouldn't have attacked her.

Samara sat up on the metal piece of slab that she called her bed for the night. The previous day replayed over and over in her mind. Her heart broke into tiny pieces with each thought. Her emotional torment was hurting her so bad, she walked through the next two hours in a daze. She was carted off to court and managed to answer the judge's questions. Her bail was set at five thousand dollars, and she was carted back to her holding cell.

When Samara got back to her cell, she ran her hands through her ponytail. Her mind raced as she thought about who she could call to help her, her sister, and friends to get out of jail. She damn sure wasn't calling Ryan. She was so mad with him that she knew if she saw his face she would get dragged back to jail for snapping his neck.

"Porter!" a raspy voice boomed. She looked over at the bars that separated her and the officer. He continued, "You've made bail."

Those words were the sweetest ones she had ever heard. She didn't know who bailed her out, but she could kiss them for doing so. Samara asked, "Did my sister and friends get bailed out too?"

"Be quiet!" the officer snapped and continued to escort Samara down the hallway. She went through the process of being released and getting her next court date. She wanted to ask if there was a phone she could use to get a ride but when they told her she could leave, she hauled ass out of the building.

"Samara." She heard her name being called. When she looked towards the voice, her girls were sitting in the back of a white Rolls Royce and Helen was leaning against the truck on the passenger side. Samara was in shock to see Helen. Helen was the last person on earth that she thought would come to her aid.

"I'm confused," Samara stated when she got in front of Helen. She interlocked her fingers in front of her body and waited patiently for Helen to turn the tables.

"You shouldn't be. I know the relationship that we had wasn't the best. Ryan is my only child and I knew that when he met you, you were everything he wanted. I'm not gonna lie, I was doing everything in my power to break y'all relationship up. When that situation happened a year ago, I had to fake like I like you, but then I realized that you really weren't that bad. I ended up liking you for real." Helen chuckled.

Samara joined in. She did notice that Helen stopped side-eyeing her and started to open up and ask Samara questions. She was just so busy with planning this bullshit ass wedding that she didn't pay attention to the change.

Helen continued, "Ryan was wrong. If this had been a year ago, I would have been defending him. Since I've grown to know you, I can't just jump to his defense and act like you deserved what my son did. 'Cause, truth be told, you don't. Not you or another woman in your situation. Get in the car and let me take you home."

For years, that's all Samara had wanted from Helen. She finally got it. And whether it was by force or not, Samara was grateful. Now she needed to figure out how she was going to deal with Ryan. Her heart hurt so bad and she couldn't think straight. Samara and her girls were quiet on their ride back home. Samara was so lost in her thoughts, before she knew it Helen was pulling into her driveway. Ryan's car was parked in the driveway. Helen cut the car off and turned toward Samara.

"Ryan is my son. Get mad, cry, scream, yell, or whatever it is you have to do in order to express your feelings to him. Just make sure that it doesn't get to the point where y'all are becoming physical."

"That is not something I am about. As angry and hurt as I am, I would never put my hands on somebody first. To be quite honest, I just want to shower this jail funk off of me and have a nice drink."

Helen nodded and said, "For what it is worth, you looked beautiful yesterday and all of the bullshit to the side, I would have been more than happy to have had you as my daughter-in-law."

Samara thanked Helen and climbed out of the car. With her heels in her hand, she walked up the stairs and let herself in. She knew that Helen told Ryan that she would handle getting her from jail. When she walked into the house, she exhaled. Hearing the TV on in the living room, she knew that's where she would be able to find Ryan. Rolling her eyes, she decided to head up to their bedroom, opting to take a shower over confronting him. As she stripped from her wedding dress, she watched as it dropped into a heap at her feet. Everything in her wanted to run out into the backyard and set it ablaze. So many emotions flooded Samara and once under the downpour of the shower head, she let her tears go. She was hurt, angry, sad, disrespected, and while she knew Raegan was a victim in this situation too, she couldn't help but feel like beating her ass again. *'She knew about me, so she ain't too much of a victim,'* Samara thought while washing her body.

Samara continued to wash her body in a daze; before she knew it, she was finished and getting dressed in the bedroom. Thankfully, it was Tuesday, the one day out of the week that her shop was closed. Her stomach growled as she thought about food. She hadn't eaten since before the wedding. Just the thought of having to go to the kitchen to get herself something to eat turned her stomach into knots. Ryan was down there and she was avoiding him for as long as she could. At the end of it all, her stomach won and she found herself making her way to the kitchen.

Her heart was set on breakfast, so she began to pull the items that she needed. Eggs, turkey sausage patties, everything bagels and grits sat on top of the table, while she moved around the kitchen placing the pots and pans where she needed them to be.

"Hey." Ryan's voice interrupted Samara's groove as she paused in the middle of flipping the patties over. Samara turned to look at Ryan who stood against the door frame, looking like a sad puppy. If her heart didn't ache, she would have busted out laughing at him.

"What?" Samara questioned with disgust on her face.

"I think we should talk," Ryan suggested.

"Oh, you think that we should talk? 'Cause I think the only person that should be talking is you."

Samara turned the stove off and faced Ryan. She wanted to give him her undivided attention, so she could hear everything that he had to say clearly. Ryan rubbed his hand down his face. He knew he fucked up in the worst way, but he never anticipated feeling the way he did. What he was experiencing was fear. He knew if he told his truth that he would undoubtedly lose Samara. But, it was now or never. He swallowed his guilt and began to spill his guts.

"Everything that Raegan said was true. I can't even begin to tell you how sorry I am. I never intended for this to happen."

"You never intended for this to happen or you never meant for me to find out?"

Ryan's head dropped as he answered, "Both."

"I can't believe this shit. How can you even stand there and say that shit? Go ahead and finish. I want to know everything. How the fuck did you not want me to find out?"

"When I met you, Raegan and I weren't together. We had been arguing a lot and I couldn't handle it. So I packed up my things and moved out. When I met you, I wasn't supposed to catch feelings. Raegan and I would be apart for months and then get back together like it was nothing. After I had been with you for three or four months, I realized that what Raegan and I had was really over. That was until you and my mother had y'all first argument. You left and

Mimi

I started drinking. Drinking led me to hitting her up on Instagram. She invited me over and I fucked her. That's all what it was supposed to be. I loved you and wanted to be with you. But I also loved her. I never told her about it until months before I proposed."

Hearing these words spill from Ryan's lips, Samara felt sick. She was doing everything in her power to keep her tears in check. She asked, "If that was the case, why not just leave me alone and be with her?"

"What I had with you, I didn't want to lose. Yes, it was fucked up and selfish of me. I know that but what me and Raegan had is done and over with."

"It should have been done once you decided to be with me! You think I'm some stupid, gullible bitch that's just going to let what happen pass and we just going to ride off into the fucking sunset! She has your fucking baby, Ryan!"

"I don't know if that's my baby and can you stop cursing at me. I'm not cursing at you and I deserve that same respect."

"You have no reason to curse at me. All of this is your fault! I have a case against me because you were with a bitch while you were with me. I was about to become your wife, Ryan! If she didn't show up, who knows how long you would have kept this shit going. And you think you deserve some type of respect. You got me all the way fucked up."

Ryan was rendered speechless. At the least, he thought that Samara would be reasonable. He didn't want to play her like a sucker so he told his truth, but the fact of the matter is, he wasn't jocking how she was handling him.

"Samara, I'm sorry. I wish I could have a plausible explanation, but I don't. I'm telling you what it was and I want to see what I could do for us to move forward."

Samara placed her hands on her hips. She was trying her hardest to keep her composure. Her supposed wedding day replayed in her mind, and she couldn't hold it in any longer. She looked at Ryan and said, "There is nothing that you can do to fix this. I don't want to move forward. In fact, I want you to pack your shit and get the fuck out. I want you to forget that you ever even knew me."

40

"You know damn well that is impossible. You have been my air, my heart, my everything for the past two years and might I add that this is my house too. I can't just erase you out of my life."

Folding her arms across her chest, her face set seriously, Samara said: "Well, then I guess that I will leave."

Ryan's heart dropped to his stomach. He wasn't expecting her to say that. He dropped his head as she walked away. Ryan was fuming and he couldn't put the blame on anybody else. Knowing there was nothing that he could do, he got up from the table, grabbed his keys and headed out of the door. He had no particular destination in mind but twenty minutes later he found himself at Raegan's house. He tried to talk himself into leaving but deep down he wanted answers. Climbing out of his car, he used his key to enter. There was a light aroma of perfume lingering in the air.

"Raegan!" Ryan called out. Moments later, Raegan walked out of the kitchen while cradling their child in her arms. She had a burp cloth on her shoulder while shaking a bottle.

"You want to keep your voice down. I just got him to stop crying. What do you want?" Raegan asked, taking a seat on the couch, placing the bottle in the baby's mouth.

"You know exactly why I am here. What would possess you to pop up at my wedding?"

"The same thing that possessed you to bring your ass here is the same thing that possessed me to pop up at that bullshit ass wedding. I want answers just like you do."

Ryan ran his hand down his face. He felt like Raegan wasn't owed any explanations. But he decided to play her game in order to find out what he needed to do. He said, "Look, I fucked up bad, Raegan. I know and I'm sorry. I was confused about my feelings and if you want me to be honest, I'm still confused. I do know that I love you but for the longest we haven't been on the same level. Before you got pregnant, I proposed to you. And what did you do? You declined and that gave me enough balls to leave our situation alone. From what you showed me, you weren't ready and I moved on."

"Ryan, you moved on without thinking about me. You didn't consider that I was going to tell you that I wanted to marry you. I've told you multiple times since we've been together that I wanted to get married. You told me to give you time. Do you know how I felt when I accidentally found a second Instagram page of yours and you posting her and bragging about marrying that bitch. I only did what my hand was forced to do."

"And what did you think that was going to do? Push me into your arms? If you thought that, you got life fucked up, Raegan. You only pissed me off even further!" Ryan stated as he took a seat on the couch. He looked over at what could be his son. At four months, he was a chunky baby. He had the same smooth hazelnut-colored skin as Ryan, and that caused a smile to spread on his face. This was his first time he had gotten a good look at the baby, and he saw a slight resemblance of himself. Ryan got up from the couch and reached for the baby.

"Are you sure?" Raegan asked. She would be grateful if he did take the baby. She could probably shit, shower, eat, and take a quick cat nap.

"Yes, I'm sure. If I'm his dad, I might as well do my part. I missed enough time and this situation isn't his fault. What is his name?" Ryan made his way back to his seat and got comfortable. Just that fast, this baby had a hold on Ryan's heart so deeply that even if the results came back that he wasn't the father, he would still act as a father figure.

"His name is Hosea. It means *salvation*. When I could no longer reach you and I was alone, he was my salvation."

"Raegan, shit ain't perfect but I'm gonna try to make this better. Go do what you need to do. I got him."

Raegan nodded and without further hesitation she ran off to go enjoy a sizzling hot bubble bath. It had been four long months since she was able to enjoy something so simple as a bubble bath. Whatever Ryan had for breakfast turned his attitude around.

Chapter Four

Two weeks passed since the fiasco at her wedding happened, and Samara had not left the house. She had told Amber and Sheeka to run her boutiques while she was enduring hell on earth. She stayed in bed, barely eating and bathing. All she had energy for was to cry, sleep, and scroll through memories of pictures and videos. She was torturing herself and she didn't realize it. All calls and texts went unanswered, the majority of them were from Ryan. He was on the top of her ignore list.

Samara slept later than usual, waking up at eleven and decided that she would get up to shower, attempt to clean up, and eat. She told herself that she was done sulking. He did what any other nigga she dated in the past would have done, and she never gave them the amount of energy she had given to Ryan. While she was ready to marry him, Ryan wasn't exempt from her return to savageness.

"Samara!" She heard her name being called. She was in the kitchen scrubbing the stove. When she turned around, Samirah was struggling with grocery bags.

"What the hell are you doing here? I told you I was fine!" Samara complained as she took a few bags from Samirah.

"Girl, your man deposited a couple of hundred dollars in my account to come make sure your funky ass had food in here."

"He is not my man and how the fuck did you get in?"

"He told me where a spare key was. What were you in here doing? When I spoke to you last night you told me that you had been confined to your bedroom for the past two weeks. Are you coming out of that funk?" Samirah asked as she placed three packs of chicken in the freezer.

Samara rolled her eyes and responded, "Two weeks was enough given to him. I'm good and ready to get back to working and living my very best single life."

Samara grabbed some cut up fruits from the fridge and popped a watermelon in her mouth. She said, "I'm going to take my time getting out of the funk."

"How is that going to work if you are still living here in his house?" Samirah asked with a raised eyebrow.

"He ain't here, is he?"

"Samara, that is disrespectful as fuck. Yes, your name is on the deed but this is still his house. I'm sure he's regretting that he fucked up but at the end of the day, that man is going to want to come home."

"And that's when I will worry about it. Ryan disrespected me. He had another woman believing they were going to be together, and she had his baby."

"We don't know that yet, Samara, so you can't know until the results are back."

Samara raised her eyebrow at her sister because obviously she hadn't seen what she saw. Another reason why she was confined to the room was because one day she decided to unblock Raegan from the page she had written Samara from. She went searching and when a woman searched, she found things. There were pictures of the two together looking like a happy couple. There was even a picture of a sleeping Ryan with the baby on his chest. They were twins. The test results didn't have to be in for Samara to know that that baby was Ryan's. With her phone in her hand, she searched for the picture she was looking for. When she found what she was looking for, she passed her phone to Samirah.

"What's this?" Samirah asked.

"Ryan with his son. I don't need a DNA test to tell me that that baby is his. And obviously Ryan didn't need it either. She posted that picture three days ago, but I know for a fact that that picture was taken the day we came home from jail."

"How do you know that?"

"When I got home he had on that same outfit. We argued and I told him to leave. He told me this was his house. So I told him that I would leave. When I said that, he changed his mind and left. I know he is waiting for the day that he thinks that I'm over it and try to waltz in here but when that day comes, be prepared to see me on your couch."

Samirah couldn't believe what she was hearing. She liked Ryan and like most men, he fucked up and she was hoping that he could fix their relationship, but she doubted that it would happen. Ryan had accepted the fact that the baby was his and was over at Raegan's house when he should have been doing everything in his power to do what he could to fix his and Samara's relationship.

"Damn, Ryan, I was rooting for you!" Samirah said out loud.

"Fuck Ryan. Fuck Raegan too and if I'm being honest, fuck that damn baby too." Samirah's mouth dropped open in astonishment. She wasn't expecting Samara to say that about the baby. She replied, "Well, damn, what the baby do?"

"Nothing." Samara shrugged. She took her fruit and went to get comfy on the couch, with Samirah following behind. Spending time with her sister seemed to do the trick with keeping her mind off of what she had going on. Ryan called and texted Samara while Samirah was there but it went unanswered.

Around nine o'clock that night, Samara suggested that they head to a local bar called *Rookie's Bar & Grill*. It was a little hole-in-the-wall bar that people frequented on Van Vranken Ave. Samirah wasn't too sure about that, being that Samara just got out of a bad situation but Samara convinced her that she would be okay. Samara didn't want to waste another night in the house. Samirah went home to change while Samara got changed at home and texted Sheeka and Amber to meet them at the bar in thirty minutes.

Before Samara left the house, she looked in the full-length mirror that was located on the wall by the front door. Thank God she didn't look how she felt. Fall was arriving, and the nights were cooler than the days. She wore a thick pair of black leggings, with a red long-sleeved crop top. On her feet, 'cause she planned on dancing all night, were black and red Jordan 13's. Everything that she was going to need for the night went inside of a black fanny pack with red zippers and a red Minnie Mouse bow with white polka dots. Her hair was split across the middle with Bantu knots at the top and shoulder-length big curl ringlets in the back. Just with lip gloss on her lips, she locked up and waited on the porch for her Uber.

Ten minutes later she arrived at Rookie's. Immediately, she noticed Amber and Sheeka standing out front; the duo were hyping each other up as they danced to the music that poured out of the bar every time someone opened the door.

"Y'all bitches are crazy as hell," Samara laughed as she made her way to the curb.

"Girl, we are just happy that you decided to bring your ass out of the house," said Sheeka.

"I'm in a good mood and I don't want to fuck it up."

Amber asked, "Where's Samirah? I like drunk Samirah, she is too lit."

Samara laughed and said: "Speaking of, she is calling me right now. Hello." Samara paused as she listened to what her sister was telling her. After telling Samirah she loved her, she hung up and turned to her friends. With her bottom lip poking out, she replied, "She got called into work."

"Dammit," Amber said.

"Well, shit, you're acting like you don't want to party with me. I'm still fun."

"Yeah, but when you get enough liquor in you, you disappear dancing with everybody in the damn building," Sheeka said with a roll of her eyes.

"Girl, shut the hell up and let's go," Samara said. They made their way inside and immediately went to the bar. They started off with two shots of Patron and decided to order garlic parmesan wings, teriyaki with pineapple sauce wings, Jalapeño poppers, and French fries to go with their whisky sours. The girls were there early enough to get a table off to the corner away from the bathrooms, speakers, and had a clear shot of the door. They danced in their seats and ordered another round of shots.

"Y'all, I'm about to head to the dance floor. Signal me when the food comes out," Samara stated. Both Amber and Sheeka always wanted to wait until they put some food in their system before they had gotten onto the dance floor. Samara liked to dance. She wasn't a professional but she had rhythm, and she could run with the best of them. Dancing was a stress reliever for her and just like any other situation where she felt like she had too much to deal with, she danced that shit away. Three songs later—and she had worked up a slight sweat and needed water. Making her way to their table to take a break, she saw Amber and Sheeka laughing at something in Amber's phone.

"Bitch, you got haters!" Sheeka yelled in Samara's ear. The video that Amber and Sheeka were laughing at played back. Samara was killing it in her zone, and there was a female posted against the bar grilling Samara up and down.

"I ain't worried about that damn girl. Y'all ready to get out on the dance floor with me?" Samara asked. Amber and Sheeka wanted to chill for the meantime. They were only there for Samara to make sure that she was straight. While they wanted to enjoy themselves as well, they both knew their girl was dealing with personal shit and couldn't let her party by herself. Cleaning her fingers with a wet nap, Samara took her glass up to the bar for a refill, making sure she stood next to the girl that was grilling her in the video. When the song *Essence* by Wizkid came on, Samara confidently made her way to the dance floor. Her waist and hips began to move in circles as her eyes rested on shorty at the bar. Samara was strictly dickly but she figured that she would fuck with the girl just a little bit. She was so busy trying to fuck with the girl that she didn't notice the presence behind her, until she noticed the girl's expression went from amusement to anger as she stormed away from the bar. As bad as Samara wanted to turn around to see who she was dancing with, she just added more sexiness to her dancing.

"Sorry for interrupting your dancing but you looked too good to let you dance by yourself," a raspy voice said in her ear. His voice reminded her of the singer Lyfe. She smelled mint on his breath and Opium by YSL on his body. The song switched, and that gave Samara the perfect chance to turn around and see who this man was. Before her stood the finest man God could have created. He stood five foot eleven inches, skin the color of walnuts, and was semi-muscular. His medium-full lips were tinted from what she assumed was from weed smoke. His hair was braided in neat cornrows to the back of his head. His beard was connected and luxuriant. When she came back to reality, Samara noticed that he was smiling. His top teeth were nice and white while his bottom row was lined with gold.

"You good?" he asked.

Samara shook her head from the fog and replied, "I'm sorry. Yes, I'm good. Oh, and I accept your apology. I think I'm going to go over to check on my girls. Thanks for the dance and it was nice meeting you."

Samara hightailed it over to her table with her friends who looked at her with confused expressions. Samara guzzled her water down as she watched the mystery man walk back to a pool table she was sure was surrounded by his friends.

"Girl, what is wrong with you?" Amber asked.

"I think I just met the closest man to God."

"Who? Where?" Sheeka asked, making it obvious by looking around.

"He's over by the pool table. The one with the cornrows. Sheeka, you making it mad hot right now."

Amber's eyes zeroed in on the pool table with the mystery man. Amber expressed: "Bitch, all them over there look like the closest men to God. Shit, let me get on this dance floor. Maybe I could finally get myself a decent man for once."

"I'm right along with you." Sheeka followed.

"I'm going to chill here for a little bit." Samara was tired and needed some water. Before she got up to go to the bar, a waitress came over with a bottle of water with another whiskey sour.

"The gentleman over there with the braids asked me to give this to you. He is also covering you and your friends' tab for the evening." The waitress politely spoke, noticing the confused look on Samara's face.

"Oh shit. Can you thank him for me?"

"Of course. He also asked me to pass this along to you." The waitress passed her a folded piece of paper and walked away with confusion on her face. Samara opened the paper and smiled when she noticed he wrote his name and number down. She was sure that the waitress would thank him for her, but she decided to text him her thanks. Almost immediately he replied.

518-237-9824: You're welcome love. Thank you for the dance. It left a lasting impression.

Samara: I don't want to store your number without asking you, how do you pronounce your name?

Ondrej: It's Andre. My pops decided to get a little creative when he chose my name.

Samara: I'm about to head out. Hit me up when you get the chance. Oh by the way my name is Samara.

Samara smiled as she put her phone in her fanny pack and grabbed her girls off the dance floor to head home. It was back to reality for Samara, where heartache had become her best friend. It was close to two in the morning when Samara had gotten home. Jumping in the shower, Samara washed away the sweat from her body and then got out. She quickly fell asleep in her towel.

The bright rays from the sun shined on Samara's face, causing her to squint as she slowly tried to open them. She was tucked under the covers as she looked out of the window into her backyard. *'Did I really leave these curtains open all night?'* she questioned. She had a lot to drink the night before, so she didn't remember. Reaching to the clock on her night stand, she saw that it was after ten. Her stomach growled as she climbed from the bed in search of some clothes. Grabbing a t-shirt from the dresser, she went into the bathroom to relieve her bladder and brush her teeth. Before she went downstairs to make something to eat, she grabbed her phone.

Absent-mindedly, Samara made her way to the kitchen. Going inside of the fridge, she took out some eggs and Jimmy Dean sausage patties.

"Good morning," a voice spoke, causing Samara to drop her phone. She was so busy looking through social media that she didn't realize a whole person was standing in her kitchen.

"Ahhh! Ryan, why would you wait to say something? I could have had a fucking heart attack!" Samara exclaimed with her hand grasping at her chest.

Ryan chuckled and replied, "I'm sorry. But the look on your face was worth it."

"What are you doing here anyway?"

A look of nervousness washed over Ryan's face. He wanted to come home, but the way Samara looked at him in disgust rendered him with nerves. Ryan cleared his throat and said, "I'm coming back home. I think it's time that we talk things out and come up with a solution because I'm tired of being away from my home."

Samara allowed a few seconds to pass as she grilled Ryan before she laughed. A good hearty laugh at that. Ryan was confused at Samara's reaction. He didn't know if he should join in the laughter or not. He chuckled lightly until Samara's face turned serious again.

"You can come home all you want. Didn't you say that this was your house too? But I'm leaving. There is nothing that we need to talk about or fix. I was loyal to you and not only did you fuck another bitch, you managed to get her goofy ass pregnant. Let me ask you this, if the shoe was on the other foot and I was the one who got pregnant, would you want me to come back and fix some bullshit?" Samara asked with her hands on her hips.

Ryan's head dropped because he knew that he wouldn't forgive her. If he was being honest, he would have kicked her out that same day. Finally he opened his mouth and said: "Nah, I wouldn't forgive you."

"Exactly. Niggas love doing the dirt but soon as it's their woman doing them the way they have been doing them, they want to tuck their dicks between their legs and act like a straight bitch about it. And you expect me to forgive you but in a hypothetical situation you wouldn't forgive me. Tuh! You got me fucked up. I'll be gone by tonight." Samara walked out of the kitchen and upstairs to their bedroom. Her stomach turned into knots as she tried to hold her tears in. She didn't like this feeling. The heartbreak was the worst feeling that she had ever felt. At any minute she thought her heart would explode through her chest. She would risk getting shot, rather than having to deal with that pain ever again.

When Samara reached the bedroom, she walked into the closet and grabbed a suitcase. She placed it on top of the bed and proceeded to move in and out of the closet, grabbing things blindly and putting them in the suitcase. She made three trips to the closet before she broke down and cried. She dropped to her knees at the edge of the bed, interlocked her fingers, and placed them on top of her head. Everything hurt Samara. Her body ached, her head ached, her stomach ached, and worse of all, her soul ached. She cried out for God to help her soul through the healing process. She had never felt so broken and she wanted it all to stop.

Five minutes later, Samara stood up from the floor, wiping her face free from the tears. She could feel the puffiness setting in on her eyes as she continued to throw clothes into her suitcase. Samara smelled him first and then his touch. Ryan came up behind her and wrapped his arms around her waist, his chin resting on top of her head. Her tears yet again fell, causing more droplets to appear on the front of her shirt.

"Please Ryan. Just go, please, so I can finish." Samara cried as she tried to remove his arms from around her waist. Despite Samara's futile attempt to remove his arms, she felt his lips against her neck, both disgusting her and moistening her lady parts. Samara knew just the kind of magic Ryan held between his legs, and she refused to allow him to even get close to her lower regions. Knowing that if he did, she would be sore a few hours later, standing at the stove cooking Ryan's dinner, while her legs shook. His pipe game was just that immaculate.

"Samara. Bae, please. I'm so sorry and it will never happen again. I fucked up badly and I am willing to do what it takes to make it up. Raegan is nothing more than my child's mother and—"

Furiously, Samara turned around because she wasn't expecting to hear him confirm that Raegan's child was his. Ryan's head dropped when he saw the hurt in Samara's eyes. Samara said: "Move, Ryan."

"No, we need to talk about this. I should have told you sooner that I found out Hosea was mine. The results just came in about a week ago. It may seem like it was a long time but I haven't even been able to come to grips with it."

Samara moved the suitcase from off of the bed and sat down. She placed her elbows on her thighs and covered her face with her hands. She calmly said, "I was going to be your wife, my nigga, and you didn't think that I needed to know that? Ryan, we shared everything together. Something like that is what you just going to keep to yourself?"

"All of those times I called you, don't you think I was trying? I could have emailed you, but you got me blocked on everything. Please tell me how I was supposed to let you know?"

Ryan had a point still. He knew where she was staying. Just like he came today, he could have popped up when he found out. But that didn't mean a thing because the deed was done. He not only cheated but he had a baby. Samara probably would have stupidly forgiven him if he had only cheated. A baby was something she was supposed to give him once they were wedded, but he threw that shit down the drain. Samara had no more words, and she was ready to leave. As she tried to stand up, Ryan moved and stood in front of her.

"Ryan, please move." Samara sighed.

"No, bae. I want to make this right. Tell me, Samara, what can I do to make this right?" Ryan asked. His voice was shaky as tears slid down his face. Ryan got on his knees in front of Samara as he made eye contact with her. Ryan would do anything she would ask of him, if that would mean that he could still exist in her world. He took her hands into his and placed soft kisses up her arms. He raised up on his knees and continued to place his soft lips to her neck. Samara whimpered because as much as her brain told her to push him away, her body missed his touch. Ryan kissed her chin, her cheeks, her nose, her eyelids, and lastly her forehead. When he pulled away from her, her eyes were closed and tears slid down her face. Ryan placed his forehead against Samara's and placed his lips on hers.

"Ryan, please—" Samara pleaded in a whisper against his lips. She didn't have the will power to move away from him; she needed for him to have it for the both of them. As soon as she felt Ryan's hands gliding up her thighs, she knew that neither one of them had the will power. Ryan's fingers graced the outside of her lace panties, causing her clit to jump in anticipation. Samara's mouth dropped open when Ryan began to move his fingers in a circular motion on her clit. Ryan leaned into Samara, placing his mouth on hers. Samara broke the kiss seconds later and laid back on the bed.

Ryan bit his bottom lip as he moved to kiss her inner thighs. Samara's back arched when she felt Ryan pull her panties from her flesh with his teeth. Ryan adjusted himself so that he could grab the sides of her panties in between his teeth, and pulled them down. Samara used her hands to cup her breasts as Ryan's fingers slid up and down her wet slit. She shivered when she felt the wetness from his tongue meet curves, and rested her hands on his head. Her hips thrusted slightly as she applied pressure on his head.

"Shit." Samara hissed. Ryan was licking her cootie cat so good, her eyes were dancing in her head.

Ryan paused, licking her kitty and inserted his index finger while his thumb rubbed against her clit. He looked up at Samara, hoping to look in her eyes. They were closed, and her hands were massaging her breasts while her thumb and index finger pinched at her nipples. Ryan's dick pumped blood as he watched the sight before him. He adjusted himself and proceeded to finger her as his tongue worked magic against her clit. Moments later, Samara was bucking her hips against Ryan's face. Her legs shook as she experienced one of the best orgasms she had ever had. Ryan didn't let up after she came. He was bricked up to capacity. Ryan spread Samara's legs around his waist and slowly slid into her wetness.

"Fuckkk, Samara. Your shit squeezing me so fucking good." Ryan whispered those words in her ear with his eyes closed. Samara squeezed her walls tighter with a smirk on her face. The Kegels that she has been doing worked wonderfully. Ryan got comfortable on his knees as he wrapped his arms under Samara's armpits and held her shoulders. He pumped his hips slowly while placing kisses on different spots on her face.

"I'm sorry, babe. I never wanted to hurt you. I love you so damn much and can't picture my life without you." Samara ignored Ryan's words; she no longer paid him any attention. She was focused on enjoying the spectacular piece of dick she was giving up. She knew that she would never have a one-night stand. Even her toys, while they worked just fine, she knew they wouldn't do any justice compared to Ryan.

"Oh damn!" Samara moaned. She was about to cum again. Ryan squeezed her body slightly and used his dick to hit her spot, causing her to erupt like she'd never done before. Her body shook, her moans were loud, and Ryan was slipping and sliding in her gushy regions.

"Fuck! This pussy is amazing. Cum for me again. I'm about to cum too. Matter of fact, turn over." Ryan jumped off of Samara, and she positioned herself in doggy. Her chest laid flat against the bed and her ass was in the air. Ryan climbed behind her waist as they caught a rhythm. Samara threw her pussy on him as she matched his strokes.

"Mmm, I'm about to cum again, Ryan." Samara moaned. Ryan picked up his pace. He was determined to cum inside of her as she was cumming on him.

"Me too, baby, me too." Ryan grunted. Samara moaned, rubbed her clit while Ryan sped his pace up. Ryan cursed and told Samara how much he loved her as he allowed his seeds to spill inside of her. Their heavy breathing was the only sound in the room, both with separate thoughts on their minds. When Ryan climbed off top of her, Samara rolled over onto her side and slid halfway under the sheet. Ryan moved behind Samara, wrapped his arm around her waist, and kissed the back of her neck. Within minutes, Ryan was snoring loudly in Samara's ear. Tears threatened to drop from her eyes. She refused to allow them to fall because she was tired of crying. She knew her heart and brain were going through a serious battle. She was afraid that her heart would win, she would forgive him, and she would have to deal with Raegan being around forever. At this point, she didn't think she could handle that.

Two hours later Samara opened her eyes. She didn't realize that she had fallen asleep. Great sex can do that to you. Ryan's snores still rang loudly as she reached for her phone on the nightstand. It was just after one in the afternoon, and Samara had things to handle before she made it to her shop. Quietly, Samara climbed out of the bed, went inside her closet and proceeded to grab some clothes. Instead of using the shower in her room and risking waking up Ryan, Samara showered in the bathroom where his parents' room used to be. When she was done, she crept back into their bedroom, grabbed her phone and eyed the suitcase she packed before Ryan pleased her body in the only way he knew how. Her eyes darted between the suitcase and Ryan. The suitcase was on his side of the bed, and she wondered if she could grab it without waking up Ryan. As stealthy as a cat, she moved slowly towards the suitcase. When she neared the suitcase, Ryan's snores stopped. Her heart pounding in her chest, she looked up at Ryan just as his snoring resumed. Samara exhaled, realizing that she was holding her breath, snatched up the suitcase, and made a beeline for the door. She moved quickly, grabbing what she needed, and flew out of the house without a second look back. Samara knew if she didn't take the suitcase, she would have a reason to come back. Putting her car in reverse, she left the house that she called home for the past two years.

Mimi

Chapter Five

Halloween was a week away and the leaves were falling rapidly, creating a sea of browns, oranges, and reds on the ground. Samara officially placed Ryan on *block* and was trying to get her life back to normal. The day that she had left Ryan's house, almost three weeks ago, she removed money from her account and paid for a hotel room for a month. She finally found her a three-bedroom, two-bathroom house located on Rosemary Drive. Her realtor was working around the clock to make sure that the transaction went fast and smoothly. Samara wanted to be out of that hotel faster than a prostitute bending over.

Samara and Amber were at work vibing with the customers while jamming to nineties' Hip Hop and R&B at her main location. Their day was halfway done, and they were anticipating the drinks they were having at Rookies with Samirah and Sheeka. This was their first time going back since Samara had met Ondrej. They texted on and off but that was the gist of their relationship. She hoped that he was there.

Eight o'clock had finally arrived and after cleaning up and filing some paperwork, Amber and Samara were on their way to Rookie's. When they arrived, the crowd was subtle. Samirah and Sheeka were already inside holding down their favorite table. Before Samara was in her seat good enough, she had downed her shot as well as Samirah's and Amber's.

"Bitch, you want these hands or nah, because what the fuck?" Amber asked.

"My bad. I'll pay for the next round. I needed it."

"You still being hard on yourself about what happened between you and Ryan?" Sheeka asked. She had her elbow on the table with her chin resting in her hand.

"No. I have come to terms with how the relationship ended. I did nothing wrong in the relationship, so I'm moving forward. Drink up, ladies."

Samirah eyed her sister. She knew Samara, and deep down, she knew that her sister was not okay. She would leave it alone for now.

She cleared her throat and said, "Well then, let's toast to new beginnings."

The girls raised their glasses and clinked them together. Once Samara downed her drink, she was on the dance floor. Grabbing their drinks, they joined Samara on the dance floor, dancing nonstop for almost an hour. By the time they took a break, Rookie's was damn near packed and they had worked up quite a sweat. Samara dragged her sister with her to the bathroom. Luckily, there wasn't a line and they each grabbed a stall.

"Girl, did you see that girl that had on that knock off Fendi outfit. Pure hot ass mess." Samirah chuckled.

"Nah, I think it was the shoes that threw the outfit off. Whether it was fake or not, the outfit was cute," Samara admitted. She finished before Samirah and she was at the sink washing her hands. The door being opened caught Samara's attention while her sister was going off about the girl's shoes. Raegan and two of her friends came in. One of them Samara recognized from her wedding day. Samara dried her hands on paper towels and eyed a smiling Raegan.

"Well, well, well. I didn't think I would run into you here." Raegan smirked while passing her clutch to her friend. Samirah exited the stall and paused when she saw Raegan and her squad standing just a few feet from her sister. Samirah sucked her teeth and proceeded to walk to the sink to wash her hands. Under her breath, Samirah said: "Not tonight, Jesus."

"Excuse me? What was that?" Raegan asked with her eyes on Samirah.

"I said, *Not tonight, Jesus*. Just 'cause you got two bitches with you doesn't mean anybody is scared. My sister will not be entertaining you or any of your antics tonight. In fact, Samara, we are leaving!" Samirah stated as she reached for Samara's hand. Samara smoothly moved away from her sister. She leaned against the sink with her fingers intertwined in front of her.

"Nah, sis. I'm with all the antics tonight," Samara said with a smirk on her face.

Raegan rolled her eyes as one of her friends said: "Raegan, you don't have to say anything to this bitch. So let's just use the bathroom and bounce. She ain't worth you spending the night in a jail cell with your son and your man at home."

Raegan placed a smile on her face and said, "Queenie, You're right. Ryan is my man and I do have his baby. Samara, is it? How come you don't have his baby? Is it because you can't carry one?"

"Is this really the argument that you want to have? I am not surprised. But let me put you up on game, sweetie. Just 'cause you got a baby by the nigga don't mean he gonna stay. If I called him up right now, trust and believe he will come running. You could sex that man so damn good and have a football team of his kids, but if he in love with someone else, he's gonna find his way home. Didn't your mama ever teach you that? Or is she the type to have a nigga baby, despite him not wanting her, just to say that she got the nigga too? You can have Ryan and I hope y'all live happily together. But in the meantime, make sure you do some Kegels and keep that pussy tight for him so he can stop calling me." To put icing on the cake, Samara held her phone up just as she felt her phone vibrating in her hand. Raegan's face dropped when she noticed that Ryan was calling Samara on FaceTime. Samara winning the fight verbally, she stepped around the trio and made it to the bathroom door with Samirah.

Raegan had one more dig at Samara. One that she knew would hurt. Raegan said, "While all of what you said was cute, I'll make sure Ryan puts your name down to send you an invite to our wedding."

Samara turned her attention to Raegan, and Samara's breath was taken away as she watched Raegan hold up her left hand. On her ring finger was the ring that Ryan gave to her when he proposed to her. She had taken it off weeks ago and because she wasn't thinking about putting it on, she never noticed that it was missing.

"Hmm. That is the exact ring he gave me!" Samara stated, watching as the color drained from Reagan's face. Samara continued and said, "It's written all over your face that you know it is. You saw the inscription on it and you still accepted it from him, just so that you one up me. But girl, as long as you wear that ring you will only look like a fool."

Samara was done playing whatever game Raegan was trying to play. Samara wasn't even mad with Raegan. Her hurt and anger was towards Ryan. In fact, she felt bad for Raegan. She was cheapening herself for a dog ass nigga that clearly didn't love her, and he was blatantly showing her that. When she made it back to their table, Sheeka and Amber were sitting there with smiles on their faces as two men spoke with them. She grabbed her purse and was about to leave.

"Wait, what's going on?" Amber asked when she noticed Samara grabbing her purse.

"I'm calling it a night. You ladies have fun and I will see you tomorrow, Amber," Samara replied.

"But I drove you here. Your car is still at the store. How are you getting home?"

Samara snorted when she heard Amber say home. What they didn't know was that Samara was temporarily living in a hotel suite. Samara said, "It's okay. That's why there is Uber and Lyft."

Without further conviction from her friends, she opened the Uber app and placed a request for a ride. Luckily for Samara there was an Uber three minutes away. She said her goodbyes to her friends and went to wait outside. Ryan had been calling her non-stop since the fiasco in the bathroom. She was positive that Raegan called him. Her Uber had arrived, and she climbed in wanting so badly to get to her suite at the Double Tree by Hilton. There was a half-bottle of *Casamigos* in her room waiting. Samara rarely smoked weed, but she kept a stash for just-in-case purposes, and she knew that she would need that too. The ride from Rookie's to the hotel was no longer than six minutes, and she couldn't have been more grateful for that. She wished the driver a safe and good night as she climbed out. The lobby was silent as she entered. She waved at the receptionist and made her way to the elevators.

Her room was hot when she made it inside. Immediately after she took her shoes off, she made a beeline for the air conditioner and set it to its lowest. With the events playing over and over in her head, Samara took a seat at the desk, grabbed her bottle of *Casamigos* and made herself a very strong drink. She reached into her duffel bag in search of her stash but couldn't find it. She became frustrated when she couldn't find it. The steady tears that streamed down her face, clouding her vision, didn't help the matter either. Throwing down her bag, she placed her head on the desk and allowed herself to cry. *For one to go through a heartbreak this bad by themselves is complete torture*, she thought. On the outside, she made it seem like she had moved on from the heartache, but deep inside she was a complete mess.

Samara allowed herself to cry for a little while longer and that was it. It was only nearing eleven at night and she wanted to forget about what happened at Rookie's. Deciding on taking a shower, she climbed in, only to find herself crying again. This was harder than she thought it would be. She could do without the constant crying. If she could get that under control, she would be fine. After Samara was done with her shower, she wrapped a towel around her wet hair and a robe on her wet body. Grabbing the bottle of *Casamigos*, she sat on the bed to carefully search for her stash. She had copped some good shit and it was calling her in the worst way. Just as she was about to give up, her fingertips graced the tube it was in. Squealing with glee, she quickly rolled a nice fat blunt and put fire to the tip. Two long hits of the exotic—and she was starting to feel the effects. Samara turned the lights off and changed the channel to enjoy some TV before she went to sleep.

Ten minutes later, Samara was crying again while watching *Sex In The City*. Mr. Big had just left Carrie at the altar, and Samara once again thought about her sham of a wedding day. Her eyes were puffy and she just knew her nose was raw from using the off-brand Kleenex that was provided by the hotel. She had a little too much to drink and she blamed the liquor for how emotional she was. Samara placed her phone on the charger and got ready to go to bed, until the chime from her phone indicated that she had a FaceTime call coming through. She hoped it was Ryan so she could give him a piece of her mind. Instead, it was Ondrej. She answered before he hung up. She knew she looked a mess and she didn't want to show her face. While her phone faced the ceiling, she peeked to look at Ondrej's surroundings and noticed he was outside.

"Hello," Samara said, catching Ondrej's attention.

Ondrej's face appeared in the camera as she said, "Hey, I happened to stop at Rookie's tonight and saw your friends. You are not partying tonight."

"No. I was there. I came back to my room because I started to get a headache."

"Let me see your face. That was the whole point of me facetiming you."

Samara chuckled before she replied, "Nah, I look busted right now."

"So."

"What do you mean, *So?*"

"Exactly what I said. Put your pretty ass face to the phone, please?" Ondrej spoke with slight aggression. Slowly, Samara picked the phone up and looked into the camera. Ondrej looked into the camera and licked his lips.

"I told you I looked busted."

A look of concern appeared on his face as he said, "Naw, you were crying. What's up? Are you good?"

"Eventually I will be. Thanks for asking."

"Can I come see you?" His face was stern and she knew that he wasn't going to take no for an answer. Maybe the company wouldn't be a bad thing.

"Sure. I am at the Double Tree on Nott Street, Room 304."

Ondrej smiled and said, "I'll be there in a few. You need anything before I get there?"

"No. I'm good. Thank you. See you when you get here."

When Samara hung up, she jumped up and looked for something decent to put on. She settled on a pair of gray tights and a black beater. She skipped the bra. Her breasts were perky enough to sit upright in her beater. She'd taken her hair down from out of the towel and shook out her damp curls. Her face still showed evidence that she had been crying, but with a shrug, she placed some lip gloss on her lips. She'd taken a gulp of the *Casamigos* to calm her nerves before she raced to the bathroom to gargle some mouthwash.

Five minutes later, Ondrej was standing on the opposite side of the door. He was dressed in black fitted jeans, black Timbs and a black hoodie. A du-rag covered his braids, and his beard was lined to perfection.

"Hey," Samara nervously said as she watched him look her up and down with a smile.

"You gonna let me in?" he asked.

"Oh shit, my bad. Come in." Samara breathed in deeply as Ondrej walked past. He smelled of a mixture of weed and *Coach for Men*. Samara could easily become putty in a man's hands just because he smelled good. Samara closed the door and told Ondrej to have a seat. She got comfortable at the edge of the bed while Ondrej proceeded to roll up.

"You want to tell me why you were crying?" Ondrej asked. Samara didn't want to talk about her issues. She hoped that he'd forgotten.

"I thought you would have let that go. Just something that I am dealing with. Going through the motions." Samara hoped that he'd accept her answer and drop it.

Ondrej's eyes held hers and read between the lines. She didn't want to vent, and he wasn't one to force someone to do something that they didn't want to do. Ondrej decided to change the subject to make Samara comfortable. He said, "You are very intriguing to me, Samara. Since I met you, for some reason I can't clear this up because some women automatically would take my statement and assume that I meant it in a sexual way."

"You must have not gotten the memo. I'm not most women. I can decipher something in a sexual sense."

"And that's why you're intriguing. What were you watching before I called you?" Ondrej asked before turning his attention to the TV.

"The Sex In The City movie."

Ondrej looked at Samara with his lip raised in a smirk. He said, "Nah, you need some cheering up tonight. Come on, you get one

63

side, I'll get on the other. We're gonna smoke this and watch something funny. You cool with that?"

Samara nodded, climbing into the bed. She was grateful that he cared enough to try to make her feel better. She was skeptical about chilling with Ondrej for the first time in her hotel room. She didn't want to give him the wrong impression. So far, it seemed like he knew how to be a gentleman. Samara was under the covers, leaning against the pillows, while Ondrej was on top of the covers. Ondrej stopped on VH1 where reruns of *Wild 'N Out* were playing. Samara loved the show and she knew it was going to lift her spirits. Ondrej and Samara passed the blunt back and forth while laughing at the antics in the show.

The next morning, Ondrej woke up to the sound of knocking. His head popped up as he looked around the room and tried to remember where he was. The weight he felt on his arm stopped him from climbing from the bed. Ondrej noticed that he had gotten under the covers and Samara was tucked under him with her head on his arm. Samara was still sleeping as the knocking continued and a little louder. *'I hope shorty ain't got another nigga sliding through. Damn, I left the burner in the car,'* Ondrej thought. Quickly and quietly, he got out of the bed to answer the door.

"Who is it?" Ondrej asked before he realized that the door had a peep hole.

"Room service. Miss Porter asked that we bring up some breakfast this morning." The voice spoke from the other end of the door. Ondrej looked through the peephole and confirmed that it was room service. The life that Ondrej lived had him always paranoid. He opened the door, and room service made his way inside. Before the man got through the door, Ondrej went into his pants pockets and gave the man a hundred dollar bill. The young black man nodded in thanks before he continued on out of the door. After closing and locking the door, Ondrej made his way to the food cart.

Lifting the lids from the spread, Ondrej revealed a bunch of breakfast items. There was buttermilk pancakes, Belgium waffles, eggs and cheese, toast, and an array of different fruits. There was a metal thermos filled with hot coffee, orange juice, creamer, and sugar. Grabbing a sausage link from the plate, he bit into it with a smile on his face. Quietly, he moved to where she was laying and brushed her hair from her face.

"Samara, wake up, beautiful." Ondrej spoke while slightly shaking her. Due to her hate for being woken up from her slumber, she grabbed the covers closer to her chin and rolled over. Ondrej laughed because he knew that feeling all too well.

"If you don't get up, I promise that I will eat all of this food by myself. A nigga hungrier than a motherfucker right now too." Ondrej joked, reaching for another sausage link.

"Okay, okay. Let me go brush my teeth," Samara said. The feeling of a hangover was beginning. Before Ondrej made it to her room the night before, she placed this order with the kitchen. She ordered enough food for four people, and she wasn't trying to figure out if Ondrej was serious or not about eating the food. With her eyes halfway open, she made her way to the bathroom. Ondrej laughed at her pained walk and surfed through the channels to find something decent to watch.

"I don't appreciate you laughing at my pain," Samara said as she came back to watch.

"Don't be so sensitive. I'm just joking with you. Do you have any pain medication that you can take to help with the headache you have?"

"No. How do you know that I have a headache?"

"The way you holding your head. You holding your neck so goddamn stiff, you making sure you don't move your head." Ondrej chuckled.

Samara side-eyed him. She didn't realize that she was making it that obvious. She replied, "You don't have to keep laughing about it."

Ondrej chuckled once more before he began to pile food onto a plate for Samara. She was grateful that even though he was being a jerk, he was also being a gentleman at the same time. In silence they ate while watching an episode of *Meet The Browns* on *BET*.

"What you got planned for today?" Ondrej asked.

"I was supposed to go help out at my store but this hangover is a guarantee for me to stay right here in this bed."

"Your store? What do you mean?"

"I didn't tell you? I own two boutiques."

"Word? Nah, you didn't tell me. That's what's up."

"They have been open for almost four years now."

Ondrej was impressed with Samara. At the moment he knew that Samara wasn't like any other female he had ever met. The women he dealt with were money-hungry and had a plethora of mommy and daddy issues. They were also fine women but they lacked something for him. He would go no further than just sex with these women. Ondrej was like your typical man. Every man secretly wanted to be in a relationship but wanted it to be the right woman. He hadn't found her yet, but Samara was making a mark on Ondrej, and she didn't even know it.

"I'm definitely going to check it out. You sell men's clothes?"

"I sell everything. Women's, children's, men's, small, plus-sized, accessories, you name it. When I opened my boutiques, I vowed to cater to everyone because not many smaller boutiques like mine would."

"You got that right. And if you do, their prices are ridiculous. I remember one time I left the crib and left my belt home. There was a boutique close to me and I decided to drop in instead of traveling all the way to the mall. Don't you fucking know them niggas charged me damn near a hundred dollars for a non-name brand belt that I could have easily paid no more than fifteen someplace else."

Samara snickered and then asked, "Who really the stupid motherfucker in this situation? You bought the damn belt when you should have just went to get one less expensive."

Ondrej eyed her from his spot and said, "Listen, I was in a rush but I learned my damn lesson. That shit won't happen again."

Reflecting on how stupid he was that day caused him to laugh. If he wasn't rushing to get to a meeting with his best friend Richie, he would have made that extra route to the mall. That was the only part of that day that was funny. When he had gotten to Richie's house, he received the worst news possible. His drug-addicted mother had died. That was his mother, so of course he was hurt, but got over it quickly. She was the reason why he and his sisters ended up in foster care. His mother was the reason that now—at age thirty-two—he didn't have any contact with his sisters. He had been trying to find them since he was thrown to the streets at age seventeen. Thinking about his sisters caused tears to well up in his eyes. He pinched the bridge of his nose and hurriedly stood to his feet.

"I'll get up with you later. I have a few things to get into today, so I'm gonna head out." Ondrej spoke as he put his plate on the rolling cart and reached for his shoes. Samara could tell that something changed his demeanor but she wouldn't ask what was wrong.

"Okay. I planned on going back to sleep anyway," Samara said, standing to walk Ondrej to the door. He wrapped his arms around her into a hug and placed his lips on her forehead. There was a brief silence and the two looked at each other, before Ondrej's cell phone rang in his pocket. They said their goodbyes and she shut the door.

"Lord, you knew what you were doing when you made that man," Samara spoke out loud. She made her way back to the bed and slept for the remainder of the day.

Mimi

Chapter Six

Ondrej pushed his red 2019 Cadillac Escalade on I-90, heading to his home in Albany. When he was leaving Samara's hotel room, Richie called him and let him know that he was calling for a meeting for their street soldiers. There was an inconvenience in their operation. Money was missing and somebody needed to answer for it. Ondrej agreed to the meeting but he needed to shower first.

Ondrej and Richie had been the best of friends since elementary. Richie had moved to Red Hook, Brooklyn when fourth grade had begun. His father was wealthy and they lived in the nice part of Park Slope. But Richie's mom caught his pops cheating and decided that she wasn't going to stay. In their prenup, it stated that if she left him for whatever reason, she had to leave the marriage with what she came in it with. That was five thousand dollars to her name. When Ms. Stacy signed the papers, she didn't think that she would ever leave him. So she signed the prenup. If she would have known that Richard Sr. was a serial cheater, she would have never signed the prenup; hell, she wouldn't have even married his ass. With the five thousand dollars she had to her name, she got an apartment in Red Hook Houses and started nursing school so that she could become a LPN.

When Richie was introduced as a new student to his fourth grade class, the bully of the class, Thomas, immediately began to torment Richie. For the simple fact that Richie was a white boy with red hair and freckles. For weeks Richie would go home drenched in milk and food from lunch, and bruises over his body. Ms. Stacy would have several meetings with the principal and Thomas' parents, but nothing changed. Until one day, the kids were at lunch and Ondrej went to the bathroom. Thomas was there with two of his friends and Richie. Richie was balled up in a corner while Thomas' friends were raining blows.

"Get off of him!" Ondrej heard himself say. He had every intention of going to pee but he knew that he had to speak up. He had enough.

Mimi

"Man, you better get your ass back!" Thomas yelled at Ondrej. Thomas was the biggest fourth grader in their school and while some were afraid to stand up to him, Ondrej wasn't. Before Thomas knew it, he was on his ass holding his hand to a bloody nose. Ondrej moved onto the next boy as he yanked him by his shoulder and gave him a two piece to his gut, instantly dropping him. Thomas was now on his feet and delivered a vicious right hook to the back of Ondrej's head, temporarily shocking Ondrej. The way they were going at it, you would have thought they were grown ass men fighting.

Now that one of the boys was off of him and the other not paying attention, Richie figured he had a chance to get some get back. Balling his fist, with all of his might, he swung and landed a vicious blow to the boy's chin, causing him to drop and hook out in pain. Thomas and the other boy were starting to handle Ondrej, and Richie panicked. Here was a stranger helping him and he second guessed himself about helping Ondrej. Without much thought he jumped on Thomas' back and wrapped his arms around Thomas' neck and squeezed with all his might. Ondrej was back on his feet and delivering blows to Thomas' friend's face. Thomas went down to his knees as he was losing oxygen. Richie jumped from Thomas' back and went to kick the other friend who was trying to get up from the floor.

"Hey, what's going on here?" a custodian questioned. He was coming to unclog one of the toilets when he heard the commotion. His voice paused the kids' movements. The custodian grabbed his walkie-talkie from his cart and radioed for school security to come and assist the boys to the principal's office. After the principal was done talking to the boys, she called their parents. They each were being suspended for a week and they were spending the rest of their day in different classrooms for in-school suspension. Ondrej and Richie were in the same class room and while they weren't supposed to talk, Richie and Ondrej did and from that moment, their friendship formed.

When Ondrej made it to his home, he parked in the garage and immediately made a bee-line for the bathroom. He wanted to

70

shower but most importantly, he needed his asshole to have a conversation with the toilet. Forty-five minutes later, his stomach felt better and he was fresh from the shower. His towel was wrapped tightly around his waist as he moved around his room getting his clothes together. Usually, for a meeting, Ondrej would have chosen one of his many designer suits. It was more than likely that he would have to get his hands dirty. Ondrej chose a pair of black Levi 511 slim fit jeans, a black t-shirt, a black hoodie, and black construction Timberland boots. Ondrej tied a du-rag around his head and threw on a black Scully to complete his outfit. He grabbed his keys, phone and wallet, and headed to his destination.

Forty five minutes later, Ondrej pulled into Brookside mobile home park. When Richie and Ondrej moved their operation from Brooklyn to the Capital District, they knew they were going to need a place to hold meetings and such. They chose the mobile park because it was small and located near wooded areas. Ondrej paid the property manager a hefty salary to turn a blind eye to whatever happened at his trailer.

When Richie and Ondrej purchased the mobile home, they gutted it out themselves and sound-proofed it. They ripped up the carpet and replaced it with tiles. Brookside had been their meeting spot for almost six years, and they thanked their lucky stars that everything had been going good. Ondrej slowly creeped down the pathway, checking his surroundings to make sure there weren't any nosey neighbors lingering around. When he was satisfied with his surroundings, he parked his truck. The light was on in the living room but everything else was dark. When they would come to Brookside, Ondrej thought it was a good idea to give off the illusion that when they were there, they should at least have one or two lights on while they handled what they needed to handle in the darkness.

Ondrej used his key to enter the trailer and walked into utter chaos. Besides himself and Richie, there was Blink, Scoop, Leon, and Tank in the trailer. Scoop and Blink were going back and forth about a bitch while Leon, Tank, and Richie were watching a late night comedy special.

71

"Bro, I'm telling you not to wife that bitch up. She is a whole hoe out here!" Blink barked at Scoop.

"My nigga, how would you know that? I just introduced you to her today. And I thought you was my nigga. Why you not supporting me?" Scoop calmly replied.

Blink couldn't believe his ears. Scoop was one of the toughest men he knew, and he was in utter shock how his friend was acting like a bitch for a bitch.

"A'ight, my nigga. I was trying to spare your feelings by trying to put you on but you leave me with no choice. Me and a few of my guys chilled with her and her peoples two weekends ago. We did them bitches filthy, and I know you saw her uncomfortable body language. She knew that I was going to tell you how she got down. Bro, you my nigga and I ain't never gonna play you like that!" Blink said. The room was quiet as everybody looked between Blink and Scoop. Several minutes later the room was rendered speechless when Scoop stood from his seat and made his way to stand in front of Blink. Scoop, with lightning speed, surprised Blink with a surprise vicious haymaker. Blink was caught off guard and stumbled. He came back with his own right hook to Scoop's chin, rattling his teeth.

"A'ight, that's enough!" Ondrej finally spoke. Whatever they were going through, they would have to figure it out on another day. Blink took his seat while rubbing his jaw and Scoop did the same, except his hand was on his chin.

"I'll let you slide with that shit, Scoop, but when you find out just how much of a THOT that bitch is and you ready to bust your guns behind that hoe, don't call me!" Blink said.

"Yeah, a'ight, my nigga."

Richie stood up, catching everybody's attention. He said, "A'ight, whatever that was about needs to be dropped. We have bigger issues here. Both Ondrej and I have chosen you all to be on the top because y'all have shown a tremendous amount of loyalty. But there is just one thing that is causing a rift in this organization." Richie spoke as he made eye contact with each one of the men. Richie was a bit more dramatic than Ondrej liked but he was his best friend and right-hand man, so he let him vibe just to get a kick out of it.

"What's going on?" Tank asked with genuine concern. Richie and Ondrej were brothers that he never had, and would stand ten toes down behind them.

"Well—" Richie began but was interrupted by Ondrej jumping up from his seat and grabbing Leon by his shirt. Leon's eyes popped in fear and his feet dangled two feet off the floor.

"Ondrej, man, what are you doing?" Leon choked out.

"Nigga, you sitting in this meeting acting like you ain't just take fifty of them thangs from me. You been my nigga for almost as long as Richie and you gonna steal from me? Fifty thousand dollars, nigga!" Ondrej looked up into Leon's eyes. When Leon heard the claims by Ondrej, fear and worry set in. He didn't know what Ondrej was talking about because he knew for damn sure that he didn't steal anything from Ondrej. He didn't have to. Ondrej made sure that his team ate, and Leon's pockets weren't hurting. Ondrej was hurt. Before he left Albany to head to Brookside, Ondrej received some information that Leon was the one who had stolen from him. If Leon needed that money that bad, he could have come to Ondrej, and with no hesitation or need for it back, he would have given it to him. That was just the way Ondrej was built.

The room was quiet due to the shock that ripped through it. Ondrej dropped Leon, causing Leon to drop to the floor. Leon gasped for air, leaving Scoop the advantage to swing a mean right hook to Leon's face, causing his head to snap back and bang against the wall. Blink followed up with a Timberland boot kick to the ribs.

"That's it!" Ondrej instructed. Leon was crumpled into the fetal position as he used his arms to cover his head. Ondrej removed the black and gold Glock 19 that rested at the small of his back. Reaching into his hoodie pocket, he removed a silencer and placed it on the gun. Ondrej squatted down, balancing his weight on the balls of his feet. Leon removed his arms from his head, ready to beg to not be killed.

"Dre, man. I don't know who pointed the finger at me, but I didn't take nothing from you, man! You know me, Dre. Me out of all people, knowing that if I needed it, you would give it to me with no questions asked!" Leon pleaded. There were tears in his eyes. As of three months ago, Leon had gotten into a financial bind due to his wife's spending habits and he ended up cutting her off. He was slowly but surely digging himself out of a hole. He thought several times about going to Ondrej but the fact that he was a husband and a father stopped him. He knew Ondrej would give it to him with no questions asked but knowing him and his pride, he would feel like less of a man.

"That's the part that's fucking with me, Leon. You know that but yet and still you stole from me."

"Ondrej, you know me better than that. Whoever told you that it was me gave you the wrong info."

Ondrej stood up and made direct eye contact with Leon. He raised the Glock, aiming the gun at Leon's head. With tears rolling down his face, Ondrej said, "If it came from somebody who didn't know you, I would have questioned it. But the fact it came from your wife makes it a lot more believable."

"Dre—" Leon was silenced with a single bullet right between the eyes. The heaviness of pain on Ondrej's heart sank to the pits of his stomach. He never thought that he would have to kill one of his best friends. Ondrej tucked the gun back into his waistband and made a beeline for the door. Ondrej had to hurriedly put Leon out due to the battle that he was having with himself. His mind told him it was the principle of the matter, but his gut—boy, his gut—told him that it wasn't Leon. Ondrej paced back and forth with his hands on his head, trying to keep his composure.

Behind him, Ondrej heard the door of the trailer open and close. The sound of crunching leaves approached him. Richie appeared next to him. He placed a cigarette between his lips and lit it. Blowing the smoke into the air, he said, "Clean-up will be here within the hour."

Ondrej nodded, not in the mood to talk. He usually stayed around to make sure that the clean-up was thoroughly done, but he couldn't bear sitting through this one. As an afterthought, Ondrej said, "I'm gonna head back into Albany. You mind sitting through this one without me? I can't believe I had to find out Leon was stealing from me from his wife. While this nigga knew the whole time I would have given it to him."

Shit wasn't sitting right with Ondrej, and he needed the space to clear his mind. He was now feeling guilty because when Richie told him that somebody from their team was stealing, Ondrej was going to dig around to see what he could find out before the meeting. To hear it from his wife, moments before he was to drive to Brookside, told him something wasn't right now that the deed was done.

"Yeah, you know I got you. You're gonna be good?"

"Yeah, bro. But something not sitting right with me."

Richie looked at Ondrej and asked, "What you mean?"

"I can't explain it. But when I can, you would be the first to know. Hit me when you get back." Ondrej dapped up Richie and walked back to his truck. Richie finished his cigarette while in deep thought.

***

Samara was busy in her hotel room folding and packing her clothes. Only after two weeks, her realtor called her to let her know that after she signed some paperwork, she could move in the next day. Her realtor faxed the paperwork to the hotel and upon signing the documents, she sent them back. Joy ripped through her body as she rocked to the music that was playing through her phone. Finally, something good had happened in her world and she was damn proud of herself.

"Can we talk for a minute? Boy, I want to know your name!" Samara belted as Ondrej's face appeared in her mind. She'd only spoken to him a handful of times since she last saw him, when he left the hotel. As she picked up the phone to give him a call, there was a knock on the door. She wasn't expecting anyone and didn't know who could be there. She looked through the peephole and on the other side of the door was a great surprise. Ondrej stood there with a solemn look on his face. Pressing her hands against her head to make sure her hair was in place, she opened up the door.

"What are you doing here?" Samara asked.

Ondrej's solemn look was quickly replaced with a smile that showed all of his teeth but didn't reach his eyes. He responded, "A nigga can't even get a hey?"

"I'm sorry. I just wasn't expecting you. Come in. How are you?"

Ondrej walked in and took a seat at the desk. With a sigh, he responded, "I'm good considering I had to bury one of my people last week."

"Oh, I'm sorry, Dre. You and his family have my condolences."

"Thank you. I really appreciate that. I came by to take you out. I need you to pick me up and I figured you would be down with some dinner and some friendly competition." Ondrej was smiling like he was planning on being sneaky.

Samara placed her hands on her hips and eyed him. Leering at him, she asked, "What kind of friendly competition?"

Dre chuckled. He said, "Just to Dave and Busters."

"Well, shit, why you didn't say that to begin with! I love Dave and Busters. Let me just finish folding these last few items and then we can go."

When Samara mentioned folding, Ondrej noticed that it looked like she was packing. He asked, "Are you going somewhere?"

"Actually, I am. My realtor closed on my house sooner than expected. I will be moving what little I have right now into the house tomorrow."

"Oh, shit! Congratulations. Now we can turn this shit into a celebration. You're gonna need my help tomorrow? What time do you need me here?"

"I don't have much. I won't need the help but thank you."

"What about the rest of your things? I know this ain't all the shit you got."

Samara laughed and said, "You right it's not. The rest of my things I have to get from my ex's house."

Dre raised his eyebrow and asked, "Is that the reason why you were crying the night I was here."

"Yeah. I had left him. He was cheating and we were going to get married."

"Don't do that."

"Do what?"

"When you speak, you hold your head high. No matter what shame and guilt that you feel, you hold your head high. I'm sorry that you had to go through that. If you need me to help you with him, I'd be more than willing to help you grab it."

"Thank you but I think I'm over with the whole situation and my ex is a lot of things but he is not going to give me any trouble. But in case he does, you're gonna be the first person that I am going to call."

"If you don't mind me asking, how long were you with him before you found out?"

"For three years. But look, I don't want to talk about that. You got an ass whooping waiting for you."

Samara threw a pillow at Ondrej and ran to put her shoes on. Ondrej called out behind her, "I'ma let you slide because you gonna receive an ass whooping so bad you gonna regret that shit."

Samara and Ondrej joked and laughed until they got to his truck. Dre was a complete gentleman and made sure that he opened the car door for her. When she was inside, she did a quick look around as Dre made his way to the driver's side. His car was nice and clean. She recognized the smell of *Febreze Gain* scented car fresheners that he had placed in his car vents. Samara's lips felt dry; she reached into her purse for her Fenty Beauty lip gloss in the Hot Chocolit shade. Reaching up, she flipped the visor down to use the mirror and a bunch of condoms, at least four of them, fell into her lap. Her mouth dropped open and Ondrej looked on with a straight face, trying to hold in his laughter. Ondrej watched as Samara picked up the condoms, applied her lip gloss and then placed them back, closing the visor.

"Shit, at least you safe," Samara replied. Dre couldn't do anything except laugh. He thought she was about to jump to a hundred on his ass, but she did the exact opposite.

"You are something else." Dre started the car and pulled from the parking spot.

"You thought I was about to go crazy on your ass. You not my nigga, so I don't expect anything from you except respect. Because I'm gonna give that to you."

Shocked by her answer, he was speechless for a few beats and then responded with: "In due time, lil' mama, that shit gonna change. In due time."

Samara hated to admit it, but she liked the sound of it. She didn't trust herself when her mouth said that she was done with Ryan. But if Dre was the move to be over Ryan, then so be it. The ride to Dave and Busters consisted of them blowing trees, listening to music at a comfortable volume, and talking about any and everything they thought of. Not wanting to ruin their high with eating first, they decided to hit up the games first. They tore Dave and Busters up, running around as if they were children. Two hours straight Ondrej and Samara went around playing games, sometimes even twice to see who could outbeat one another. Samara didn't notice but Dre did. The staff had been watching them closely, so to avoid any altercations where he would act a fool, after their last game, he let her win and they went to the dining area.

Upon being seated, their waitress handed them their menus. Dre was driving and decided not to drink, while Samara ordered two glasses of the *Perfect Patron* margaritas. When the waiter left to get their drinks, Samara had a feeling of nervousness wash over her.

"You okay?" Dre asked, catching onto her changed demeanor.

"Yeah, I think I just got a little dizzy."

"You want some water?"

Samara shook her head and replied, "No, I should be fine."

"Okay. Now that's out of the way, I would like to know about your family. If I am overstepping any boundaries, please let me know."

"I have no problem with letting you know if you do want to know. This mouth has no filter. Speaking about my family is always a touchy subject for me. However, I'd rather speak about them early on, just to get that part over with."

"It sounds like you don't have a good relationship with your family."

The waiter came back with their drinks and took their food order. Samara went with the fire-grilled salmon that came with Jasmine rice and garden-green bean medley, while Ondrej went with the fire-grilled sirloin, bacon wrapped shrimp, and lobster sauce. It was served with green beans and garlic mashed potatoes.

"Mm. I hope that you got some gum or mints in the car 'cause your shit gonna be kicking by the time we leave out of here!" Samara joked.

Ondrej chuckled and replied: "Oh, you got jokes. A'ight, I'm gonna get you back. But for right now I want to know about your family."

Samara playfully rolled her eyes. She was slightly amused that he didn't forget where he was at. Samara took a sip of her drink and exhaled. She began, "I have an older sister and a younger brother. My parents were together up until my mom became pregnant with my brother. I was about nine at the time and Samirah was thirteen. My mom caught my dad cheating and they split. When my mom had my little brother, he was born with cerebral palsy and was the sunshine to myself and my family."

Talking about her brother and parents was always a soft spot for her. Pausing before she continued, willing herself not to cry, she took one last deep breath and exhaled. She continued, "On my little brother's ninth birthday, we were having a barbeque for him. There were people everywhere in our front yard enjoying themselves. My mother, father, and Sage were dancing together to his favorite song 'Happy' by Pharrel. Sage, despite having cerebral palsy, was by far the shiniest star in a world that was—is so damn dark. The music was thumping through the speakers, but no one couldn't miss the sound of screeching tires. Time seemed to slow down. A woman jumped from the car screaming and yelling at my father. She kept yelling that my father needed to leave with her. That because he was with her, we were no longer his family.

"When the music stopped and people were beginning to be nosy, I made my way from the porch so that I could grab Sage. She had a gun. She shot my brother and my mother. As the woman fled, everybody was frantic. She'd shot my brother in his face. My mom was shot in the neck. She died at the hospital. While my mom and Sage were being taken away, my dad went after the woman. She stupidly went back to the apartment that they had shared. When my dad got there, from what the neighbors said to the police, they heard arguing and some glass breaking. Which ultimately led to them hearing a gun discharging twice. My father took his life right after he took that woman's life."

Samara cursed at herself in her thoughts. The moistness that was on her face angered her because every time that she would talk or think about that day, she felt guilty for not doing much to save Sage. Samirah was in the house at the time, preparing to bring the food outside. She didn't have to worry about nightmares waking her in her sleep. Samara still had some nightmares but therapy had been working wonders. Ondrej's touch to her face brought her back to reality. Ondrej had used some napkins and patted her face dry.

"I'm sorry that you had to go through that. Seeing one of your loved ones being killed in front of you, I'm sure, is devastating. And I understand. I have had so many of my loved ones murdered and one thing for sure is that dealing with the situation gets easier."

Samara smirked. She was surprised that he was so attentive. She definitely wasn't expecting it. She replied, "Thank you."

"Nah, no need to thank me, beautiful. I appreciate you opening up to me."

The waitress appeared and placed their food in front of them. Their conversation flowed naturally for the remainder of the night. By the time they were done eating, Samara's face hurt from laughing and smiling so much. Samara didn't think she would enjoy the night as much as she did. He was the perfect gentleman, from opening the door for her, to paying for everything, and then last but not least, when they made it back to her hotel room, and he asked her if she was okay if he kissed her. Without hesitation she nodded and almost melted right in his hands once his lips were on hers. He still had a tad bit of garlic on his breath, but she didn't mind. The kiss was perfect so much so, she almost came right then and there. Samara thought about asking him if he wanted to come in. His phone ringing interrupted. The call was short but so was their night. Ondrej pulled Samara in for a hug. With the promise of calling her the next day, Dre left, leaving Samara with a soaking wet pussy.

Mimi

Chapter Seven

"Bitch, this house is fucking nice!" Samirah said excitedly. Samara was moving into her house finally. Everything that she had in her hotel room was able to fit inside of her and Samirah's car. She was planning on stopping at Ryan's house later in the day to grab whatever else she needed to grab.

"I know. I fell in love the minute I stepped through the doors," Samara stated. The house was very spacious with four bedrooms, two and a half bathrooms, floor-to-ceiling windows, a dining room, and a finished basement. The kitchen was supplied with stainless steel appliances, an island in the middle of the room.

"Don't be mad when I move in."

"No, ma'am," Samara replied. "I want my peace and quiet. I dealt with Helene for two years when she was being a bitch. I need my peace."

"When are you going furniture shopping?"

"Shit. I don't know. I'm getting the rest of my clothes from Ryan's as soon as I shower and change. Might as well do it now while he's at work so I don't have to see him."

Samirah finished off her glass of orange juice and informed her sister that she was going home to nap before work. After Samara made sure that her door was locked and her alarm set, she made her way into her room to enjoy a nice hot shower. Her body was sticky from her sweating, and a hot shower was needed. While she was in the shower, she exfoliated her body thoroughly.

Twenty minutes later, she climbed out of the shower smelling like freshly picked roses. Wrapping a towel around her body, she proceeded to look through her suitcase for an outfit. She settled on a pair of black *Pink* sweat pants with the logo etched at the bottom of the pants, a white long-sleeved *Pink* shirt, and she would place her brown Uggs on her feet. She placed her hair in a low ponytail, grabbed her keys, phone, and her shiny black cropped bubble coat, and left her house. She only lived about fifteen minutes from Ryan. As she drove, her stomach tightened in knots. She figured he was at work but there could always be a possibility he decided to stay home. It would be her luck that he was there. She was relieved to see that his car was gone.

"Let me make this quick. I just hope he didn't change his locks," Samara said aloud to herself. Climbing out of the car, Samara looked for the right key on her key ring, and made it to the door. Relief washed over her when the key turned in the lock and the door knob twisted. Hurriedly, she entered the house and briskly made her way to the bedroom she once shared with Ryan. At a quick glance the room looked like nothing had changed. Going into the closet, she grabbed her other luggage set and began to throw her things inside of them. Thirty minutes later, she had two garbage bags and was preparing to put her shoe boxes inside.

"What the fuck you doing in my house?" came a voice that both startled and annoyed her. Samara was bent over at the waist but straightened up when she heard Raegan's voice.

"Your house? Last time I checked, my name was still on the deed. You better go on ahead, let me get my shit, and leave me alone."

"I live here and you are not getting shit. How the fuck did you get in here anyway?"

Samara was trying her best to ignore Raegan. She had already been to jail for this broad; she wasn't trying to go back again. Samara turned her back to pick up the next box of shoes to place in the bag when Raegan walked in front of her and slapped the box from her hands, causing Samara's blood to boil.

"I said you're not taking shit from this crib. You can come back when Ryan gets back or if you have a police escort."

"You know that you don't want me to come back when Ryan is here. You and I both know that he would forget that you are even here. Girl, move out my way before I dog walk your ass around this house." Samara glared at Raegan for a few seconds before she reached for the same box. Raegan, feeling bold and confident, slapped the box out of Samara's hands again. Before Raegan knew it, Samara came up with her fist balled and landed the blow to her chin. Raegan stumbled and then fell on her ass, and Samara wasn't going to take advantage of that. She wanted to make sure that Raegan saw each blow.

"I'm calling the cops!" Raegan yelled while holding her chin.

"Bitch, call them! In the eyes of the law, you're gonna be the one being dragged out in handcuffs. Now get the fuck out of my way!"

Samara hurriedly began to place the shoe boxes inside of the bags. It was taking everything in Samara to be the bigger person. She was working on some deep breathing when she heard Raegan on the phone yelling that there was a burglar in her house. *'I'm not about to play with this bitch. Let me get my shit and get gone,'* Samara thought to herself. One by one, Samara threw her suitcases down the stairs and went back to grab her two bags of shoes. Raegan was now on the phone with Ryan and yelling that Samara was taking things from the house. Samara made her way to the door and Raegan jumped in front of her, slamming the door shut. Samara had had enough. She dropped the bag of shoes and sent two piece shots to her gut, instantly folding Raegan.

"You know damn well you can't fight but you keep asking for an ass whooping." Raegan rushed Samara and tackled her to the ground. Raegan sat on top of Samara and swung her fists, trying her hardest to connect with Samara's face. Raegan fucked up when she paused to catch her breath. Samara grabbed her by her shirt and slammed Raegan off of her. Samara grabbed Raegan by her hair and slammed her fist into her face.

"Get off of me!" Raegan yelled while kicking her feet wildly.

"Nah, bitch. You wanted to act bold. You about to accept this ass whooping. I'm not gonna keep telling you!" Samara yelled.

Bang! Bang! Bang!

"Schenectady County Police Department! Open the door now!" police officers yelled. Samara was too far gone seeing red. She didn't hear the warnings from the officers at the door. Samara let Raegan's hair go and was now kicking her. The door to the house flew open and officers spilled into the room and tackled Samara to the ground. She was immediately placed in handcuffs to get her to calm down.

"Pussy ass bitch! This ain't your fucking house!" Samara yelled back once she was picked up from the ground. The officers separated the two women. Samara was placed on the couch while Raegan was taken into the kitchen. For ten minutes the officers asked the right questions, but both women's stories didn't add up. Trying to figure out who was the culprit, they decided to take both of them to the police station and figure it out from there. Helen walked in right before they were to put the cuffs on Raegan.

"Excuse me? What is going on here? Samara what happened?" Helen asked, drawing attention to her.

"Ma'am who are you?" an officer asked Helen.

"This is my son's house. Who is in charge here?"

A tall dark-skinned handsome dude stood forward and said, "I am. My name is Captain Turner. You are?"

"Helen Mumford."

"According to Ms. Porter, she lived here with Ryan Mumford until she found out that he cheated on her with the woman in the kitchen, Ms. Raegan Gamble. Ms. Porter says her name is on the deed but Ms. Gamble says that Ms. Porter is lying."

"So why hasn't anyone thought to check the deed?" Helene asked while she folded her arms across her chest with sass.

"Ms. Gamble said she doesn't know where Ryan had it and Ms. Porter is claiming she doesn't know where it's at either."

Helen rolled her eyes and looked at Samara who sat with a smirk on her face. Helen said, "Is it in the same place that it always has been?"

"Yup," Samara responded.

"I'll be back. It's upstairs in his office."

Captain Turner instructed one of his men to follow Helene upstairs. Helen made her way to her son's office. In his drawer, at his desk, was a pin-coded safe. Helen entered her birthday and the safe popped open. Locating what she needed, she and the officer went back down to the living room. Helene handed the deed over to the captain.

"Uncuff her!" the captain demanded, pointing at Samara.

"I told y'all from the beginning that this was my house. If your damn officer didn't tackle me to the floor the way he did, this would have gone smoother.

"Ms. Gamble, you have to gather your things and leave." Captain Turner said, disregarding what Samara said.

"What? Why do I have to go?" Raegan asked. She looked at Samara who stood behind the officers, childishly flipping Raegan off with her tongue hanging out.

"I have the deed right here, ma'am, and your name isn't on here."

"She assaulted me!" Raegan shrieked.

"You are trespassing on her property. She's had every right to protect her home. You just be lucky it was just a fight. Most homeowners have weapons and this could have ended worse."

Raegan came to the realization that she had lost. She began to gather her things and headed to the door. She paused in front of Helene. Helene liked her, so she was confused as to why she didn't speak up for her.

"Helene, tell Ryan that he can always see his son, but this was the last straw." With her head held high, Raegan left with the police officers. Samara got up and began to gather her things up.

"Long time no see, Samara." Helene spoke while taking a seat on the couch.

"I know, Helene. I've been trying my hardest to disassociate myself from anything that has to do with Ryan."

"Shit, I ain't did shit to you."

Samara glared at Helene, causing her to change her answer. She continued, "Not since that day you set my ass straight. Don't be a stranger. You were almost my daughter-in-law and I don't want that to change. I don't know about you, but I cherish the relationship that we have now."

"I do. All I ever wanted was for us to get along. I promise that I won't allow this to fuck that shit up," Samara stated, walking over to Helene to pull her into a hug. She needed to go home and shower. She wanted to start unpacking as well, but her body was already starting to ache.

"You didn't have to do that girl like that. Her baby still got to look at her in the face," Helene said with a sly smirk on her face.

"Helene, you should already know I don't give two shits. Let me get up out of here. When I get settled into my new house, I'll give you a call for brunch."

"Sounds like a plan."

With one last hug, Samara grabbed her things and in two trips, her things were in her car. She looked in her rear view mirror and she noticed her hair was all over her head and there was a long scratch, from her eyebrow going diagonal across her nose and stopping at the corner of her mouth. Sucking her teeth, Samara put her car in drive and backed out of her parking spot. On her drive home, Samara was lost in thought about the fight. Bitches like Raegan is what makes Samara stay to herself. She had severe anger issues growing up, and she worked her ass off to get to where she was at, and she hated when people took her to that level.

"I don't even feel like I dog-walked her ass enough. Bitch needs to learn to leave me alone when I say *leave me alone*!" Samara said aloud. Samara pulling up to her new house put her in better spirits. She couldn't wait to walk through her doors and pop open a bottle of *Ace of Spades Brut Gold*. After the day she had, she needed to decompress with a bottle of wine. Grabbing the two biggest suitcases from her trunk, she went inside her house. Taking her shoes off at the door, she set her alarm and made her way into the kitchen. Going into the fridge, she grabbed her bottle of wine and sat on her island.

Ping! Ping!

Samara's phone rang, letting her know she had an incoming phone call. Sighing, she took the phone from her pocket and answered.

"What it do, baby?" Ondrej's voice rang through the speaker, instantly causing Samara to smile.

"Hey, you. What you up to?" she asked, sipping from the bottle.

"Nothing much. What you doing in about two hours?"

"I'm probably going to be drunk and unpacking."

"Oh, yeah, that's right. You moved in today. Well, that gives us something to celebrate. But look, I'm running around and won't have time to stop at my spot. Do you mind if I take a shower and get dressed there?"

"Firstly, I didn't agree to going out. But since I do feel like celebrating this occasion, I will. And yes, it's fine. Just let me know when you are on your way so I can disarm the alarm and unlock the door."

"A'ight. I should be on my own in about an hour."

"Are you going to tell me where we are going?"

"Nah. I'll hit you back in a little bit." With that, Ondrej banged it on her. She would be lying if she said that his slight aggression didn't turn her on. Biting her bottom lip while smirking, instead of unpacking, Samara went to her car and grabbed her portable speaker. Upstairs in her room, a massive one at that, she planned on putting a king-sized bed as soon as she started furniture shopping. Turning her music on, she went through her boxes, looking for the perfect outfit. It wasn't as easy as she figured it would be. She didn't know where he was taking her. By the time she got out an outfit together, Ondrej was on his way.

Samara had disarmed her alarm and unlocked the door before she went inside of the kitchen to pour him a glass of Ace of Spades, before she finished the rest of the bottle. Ondrej was impressed when he walked inside of the house. After he locked the door, he looked around the foyer. There was a Swarovski crystal trimmed chandelier hanging from the high ceilings. To his right was what could have been a den, and behind that was the dining room.

"I'm in the kitchen!" Samara called out. Following where he heard her voice coming from, he found himself walking down a long hallway and made a left. He passed a bathroom. About twenty steps later, he noticed that to his right was a beautiful kitchen. The large windows let in natural light, a marble countertop island stood in the middle of the room where the sink and glass top stove was located. In the far right corner was a walk-in pantry; to the left sat the fridge, and there was plenty of counter space. After a quick sweep of the room, his eyes landed on Samara. She was leaning against a counter with two glasses of liquid in her hand. He noticed the bottle of Ace of Spades on the counter and he smiled.

"You like?" Samara asked, walking his glass over.

"I do. This shit is dope as hell." Ondrej took a sip from his glass.

"Thank you. My realtor did a fucking amazing job finding this gem."

"Shit! You might have to send them my way. When you going to get furniture?"

"I planned on doing it tomorrow. It's only been a day since I moved in and I'm dreading sleeping on an air bed."

Ondrej licked his lips and said, "You're more than welcome to sleep in mine until you get yours."

Playfully, Samara rolled her eyes while responding, "I bet. Anyway, where are you taking me? I need to know how to dress."

"I'm not telling you. Go with your gut while dressing. I forgot my bag in the car. I noticed I passed by the bathroom when I came in here. Go start getting ready."

When Ondrej departed from the kitchen, Samara couldn't help but smile. She liked when he spoke with authority. Filling her glass up, Samara walked out of the kitchen and upstairs, knowing that her panties were wet. Samara heard when Ondrej came back in as she headed into her master bathroom. Setting the water to her preferred temperature, she began to disrobe. The hot water beat down on her body, causing her to moan in satisfaction. Samara reached for her coconut milk exfoliating body scrub. She applied it all over her body, quickly shaved what little hairs she needed gone, and then washed in her favorite coconut and shea butter body wash. Samara climbed from the shower and placed a towel around her body. Inside of the bedroom, she looked at the different outfits that she picked out for the night. She was stuck between a long-sleeved multicolored dress that clung to her body and stopped at her knees, or the black distressed high-waisted jeans and a red button-up blouse that had puffy sleeves. She settled for the dress, which she accompanied with a pair of lace-up chunky heel booties.

Samara let her pin curls down and shook them loose once she was dressed. Running her fingers through her curls, she decided against make-up but as soon as she was to get downstairs, she was going to apply lip gloss. Before she left her room, she spritzed on *Eros Pour Femme* by Versace.

"You ready?" Samara called out as she walked down the stairs. He wasn't in the living room, so she started towards the bathroom.

"Yeah. I'm just checking the fit!" Ondrej called from the bathroom. Samara opened the bathroom door and walked in, finding Ondrej clad in black jeans, a white knit turtleneck. The wrists on the sleeves and the bottom of the shirt had *Dior* stitched in white on a black background across his chest. Two diamond Cuban link chains rested around his neck. One of them held an iced out lion's head with a crown and ruby eyes. She realized that she was staring at him and snapped back to reality, catching Ondrej doing the same thing.

"Damn, girl. I wasn't expecting you to come down here looking like that," Dre spoke.

"You're not telling me where we are going. Do you think I'm overdressed? Should I change?"

Ondrej looked at Samara up and down and smirked. He said, "Nah, you good."

Samara blushed while Ondrej turned around and faced the mirror. She noticed Ondrej reaching into his bag and retrieving a bottle of cologne. Quickly, Samara held her hand out, stopping him before he took the top off.

"What's good?" Ondrej asked, facing her with concern in his eyes.

"What you about to do?" Samara asked.

"Put cologne on," Ondrej said, confused.

Samara dropped her shoulders and paced back and forth. She looked at Ondrej and said, "I know that's not *Dylan Blue* by Versace.

Ondrej looked at Samara in confusion. He asked, "What's wrong with it? You don't like the way it smells? I don't have to wear it."

"When I was growing up, my uncle always told me to avoid men who wear *Dylan Blue*. He said they were fuck boys. It was a stupid theory from my uncle that I never paid attention to. Until every man that I met who wore *Dylan Blue* was a fuck boy. Please don't tell me that you're a fuck boy. 'Cause I like you." Samara's hands were on her hips. Ondrej stood in awe at what the woman standing before him said.

"Your uncle is a fucking hater, and those niggas wasn't like me. I can tell you all day that I'm not a fuck boy and what do you think that's gonna do? My actions are what's gonna show you that I'm not. Now that I know your reason, I'm gonna wear it and your uncle can kiss my ass."

Ondrej turned back to the mirror and opened the spray bottle and spritzed on the cologne. Samara couldn't help but smirk at Ondrej's response. She turned around and made her way inside of the living room. She grabbed her black waist length, shiny puffer coat from the closet and grabbed her clutch. Two minutes later, Ondrej came from the bathroom looking and smelling delicious. A smirk displayed on his face as he walked closer to Samara by the front door.

"Are you ready to go, pretty lady?" Ondrej asked, his eyes taking in every inch of her face.

"I am."

Ondrej swiftly wrapped his fingers at the base of her neck while his thumb caressed her jaw bone. He leaned in and placed a kiss onto her chin. Her pussy throbbed from his closeness.

"Let my actions speak for themselves before you start judging. Okay?" Ondrej asked. He liked Samara and he hoped that one day he could meet her uncle and give that man a piece of his mind. He watched as Samara nodded. Ondrej licked his lips right before he placed his mouth over hers. The kiss was short and without tongue, but Samara was almost positive that she was about to melt. Ondrej opened the door for Samara. They climbed into his truck and made their way to Prime 677 in Albany. There they enjoyed dinner and wine while getting to know each other.

Chapter Eight

The sound of the doorbell ringing sent Samara rushing to the door. She was expecting her sister, Amber, and Sheeka to come over to help her shop for furniture. It had been two days since she had dinner with Ondrej and was planning to go to dinner with him after she was done shopping with her people. Ondrej was the perfect gentleman. They had dinner, had great conversation, laughter, and then he took her home. She just knew that they were going to hump, but he told her that he had some business to take care of. Him taking her out that night was his way of apologizing and making it up to her.

"Yes, can I help you?" Samara asked the man that stood in dusty black jeans, work boots, and a black coat. He had a clipboard in his hands.

"Are you Samara Porter?" he asked, looking down at the clipboard.

"Yes, I am."

"I have a delivery and a note for you. We have a king-sized bed and dresser set. Where would you like it?"

Stunned, Samara gave the man instructions on where to put it. The delivery man handed her a note and went back to his truck, then he and his helper started to unload the truck. While the men worked upstairs, Samara stood there in the living room, reading the note:

Samara,
This is just a small token to show you my appreciation for understanding that I had to cut the night short. Can't wait to see you tonight.

Ondrej

Samara couldn't help but smile after she read the note. Ryan had been the only other man to gift her things, and she thought that she would never find that quality in a man again. Ondrej didn't know that he just earned himself some brownie points.

"Hola, bitch!" Samara heard Sheeka yell from the living room.

"I'm in the kitchen."

"You might want to come here. There's a delivery guy here."

While walking to the living room, Samara said: "I know, girl, I already let them in."

"Are you Samara Porter?" the masculine woman at the door asked.

"Yes, I am. Hold up, I'm confused."

"Ma'am, we are on a tight schedule. May we come in to bring in and set up this delivery?"

"Um, yeah, sure," Samara responded, looking at Sheeka, confused.

"Oh, yeah, this is for you." It was another envelope, and Samara couldn't help but blush. The note was a simple: *'Oh you thought I was done lol.'* In walked the delivery people with a living room set, complete with a sixty-five inch television.

"Bitch, is this stuff from that dude you met at Rookies?" Sheeka asked. They made their way into the kitchen.

"Yes."

"Damn, bitch, what you got between your legs? I need your fucking secret."

Samara sipped from her glass, winking at Sheeka. She responded, "I haven't even let him get a whiff yet."

Sheeka's mouth dropped open. She couldn't believe that her friend had a nigga dropping big coins on her and he hadn't even gotten close enough to smell her twat. If anybody asked—and if Sheeka had to be honest—she would admit that there was a bit of jealousy residing in her. But nobody asked, and Sheeka vowed to take that shit to her grave.

Samirah and Amber walked into the kitchen rubbing their hands together to speed up the warming process. Samara embraced her sister and Amber, giving them a hug and poured them a glass of champagne.

"Why didn't you just call to tell us that you already did your shopping?" Samirah asked as she watched delivery people move about her sister's house. There were people in every room of the house putting together bed frames, dressers, tables, curtains, couches, etc.

"Because I didn't know that Ondrej was going to furnish my whole house. He said this was to go with his apology for cutting our night short the other night." Samara smiled.

"Wait, hold up. He had to cut y'all little date short and he furnished your whole house as a part of an apology? What kind of magic you got, sis? We blood so we should have the same goodness between our legs but bitch ain't no nigga was this thoughtful."

The girls erupted in laughter. Sheeka said, "I said the same thing but Mirah, your sister ain't let him get that close."

Samirah's eyes ballooned open as she gawked at her sister. She asked, "How did you do it?"

Samara laughed, held up the peace sign and replied, "I'm just a vibe."

The conversation quickly moved to something else. With the music blasting, the women talked and joked amongst themselves. Before they knew it, four hours had passed, every room was cleaned and set up, and the women were sweaty. The delivery people had been long gone, and the sun was soon to set. As the women sat around the living room, the doorbell went off.

"Who the fuck is it now?" Samara grumbled as she got up from the couch. Her muscles ached and she couldn't wait to soak in a hot bath with Epsom salt and lavender bubble bath.

"Who is it?" Samara asked when she got to the door.

"Girl, open this door." It was Ondrej. Immediately, a smile spread on her face. She unlocked the locks and opened the door.

"What are you doing here?"

"Christmas is coming in three weeks and I knew you didn't have a tree. So I figured we could decorate it together after dinner," Ondrej said. He felt silly for even doing this, but there was something about Samara that made him want to show this side to her. He watched as Samara's lips turned upward, smiling.

"Aww, Dre. Hell yeah, I'm down. Aww, that's so sweet." And she wasn't lying. She did think it was sweet. It was a small gesture but she found it romantic.

Ondrej exhaled in relief. He said, "A'ight, let me go get the stuff from the car. I still gotta go get a haircut and get ready. Oh and this is a double date tonight. You get to meet my best friend."

"Oh, so that's why you did all this? To butter me up?" Samara laughed.

"Nah, it was a sincere apology for the other night."

"You furnish all female houses that you owe an apology to?"

Ondrej smirked and walked closer to Samara. He pecked her lips and replied, "Only the ones that I feel like they are worth it."

With that, Ondrej walked back to his car as Samara went back to the living room with her girls. They were about to grill Samara about who was at the door, but then Ondrej walked in behind Samara with an eight foot tall Christmas tree. They all exchanged hellos, and Ondrej continued to bring in the decorations. There was light conversation but it was only so Samara's friends didn't hound Ondrej. She knew they had questions for him, but that wasn't the moment it needed to happen.

Ondrej walked to the back of the couch that Samara sat on. He leaned down to Samara and said, "The house looks great. I'm gonna call you when I'm on my way."

"Can you tell me where we are going this time?" Samara asked with a laugh.

"Yeah. *The Nest.* I heard the food is good."

"Okay. See you soon, handsome." Ondrej leaned in and placed a kiss on her cheek and then her lips.

"Aww." Her girls swooned. Ondrej left with a shake of his head.

Sheeka was the first to speak. "Girl, I don't remember him looking that damn fine. He has brothers?"

"No, just sisters. He does have a best friend, whom I am meeting tonight apparently. But he is bringing somebody. However, I don't know how serious it is."

"Well, shit, if it ain't serious, send that nigga my way."

Samara chuckled and responded, "I got you."

Samirah turned to Samara and spoke. "Sis, I can see that you are feeling Ondrej and I love that for you. I just want you to take things slow with him. You kind of moved fast with Ryan and I don't want your heart broken again."

"Trust me, Mirah, I'ma be okay. I know what red flags to look for and so far, Dre doesn't have them. The only thing is that he wears *Dylan Blue*."

Samirah gasped loudly and said, "That is a huge red flag. What do you mean?"

Amber interrupted and asked, "Wait, what does that mean? What's wrong with *Dylan Blue*?"

"According to our Uncle Rory, if a man wears *Dylan Blue*, it means he is a fuck boy. Uncle Rory always warned us about it, and this fool learned the hard way and had two niggas she was in a relationship with that were fuck boys."

"So you think Dre is a fuck boy?" Sheeka asked.

"Honestly, I don't. I flipped out a little when I saw him about to put it on. He told me to trust his actions and I'm going to do just that and as soon as I see something different, I'm running like a track star."

"Well, bitch, I'm about to get up out of here. Make sure you suck the skin off that nigga dick. That man furnished your whole house without even tapping it first!" Sheeka said.

"Sheeka, just because Dre gifted me something doesn't mean that I need to give him some. When we have sex it's because we were in the moment. I'm a lady, not a whore."

"Well, shit, call me whoriana because let a man gift me some nice shit, and at that same moment I'm dropping to my knees. What Lil Kim said, *'I used to be scared of the dick, now I throw lips to the shit, handle it like a real bitch.'* "

The room erupted in laughter. Sheeka had no problem with speaking her mind. Sheeka loved sex and didn't give a fuck about speaking her mind when it came to the topic. However, Samara thought that at times it could be too much. She loved her friend, but she needed to let her know that her worth is more than just sexing niggas because they bought her something. After the cackle they had, Samara's girls left. She was now alone and could actually take in what Ondrej had done for her. She started in the living room.

Mimi

The living room set was a gray sofa and loveseat set. A large gray rectangle shaped ottoman sat in the middle of the floor on top of a light gray rug. The side tables were wooden, painted in black. The TV was mounted over her fireplace, and gray curtains hung from the windows. She entered the dining room in awe. On top of a burgundy and gold rug was a round marble top table. It was more black than white. The chairs, on the outside, were black and the fabric on the inside was burgundy. The guest bedroom downstairs had a queen-sized bed, equipped with a dark brown bed frame, dresser, and night stands. The other two guest rooms looked like the first. All she had to do was get comforter sets for them.

She saved her bedroom for last. Her breath was caught in her throat. She left Samirah the task of setting up her room. Samirah knew her best, and how Samara would like it set up. The king-sized bed sat between two windows. The head and footboards were tufted, accented with silver buttons. The fabric was a velvet navy blue. Navy blue and white curtains adorned the windows. Her pillows and comforter set matched the curtains with the blue stitched into the comforter in intricate flower designs. A silver colored dresser with a mirror sat against the wall to the left of the bed. To the right was a vanity the same color as the dresser. A sixty-five inch TV was mounted to the wall in front of the bed. There was still a ton of space in her bedroom, and her mind was working overtime at how she was going to fill up the space.

When she walked into her massive closet, she noticed Samirah had hung her clothes up, but there were a few outfits laid out on the vanity bench. Samara appreciated the thought. Samirah had been such a blessing to Samara throughout her life. After the passing of their parents, Samirah stepped up and took on the mother role. While Samara looked over the outfits, she thought about how fast Christmas was coming, and thought about how she could get her sister to show her appreciation. A thought popped into her head as a smile spread across her face. She chose the middle outfit, telling Samara it was her favorite. After grabbing her accessories and shoes, she took a nice hot shower. She went in smelling like all types of sweaty locker room, and emerged smelling like cocoa mango *Dove* body wash.

Samara quickly applied lightly scented body butter after she realized Ondrej would be coming to get her in thirty minutes. She quickly placed her legs in the acid-wash high waisted jeans, and put on a pink long-sleeved blouse with peek-a-boo shoulders, and floral print six-inch heels that tied at the ankle. There were pops of pink, blue, and gold throughout the pattern. Samara brushed her hair into a low ponytail, put on her diamond bangles, grabbed her things, and made her way downstairs.

Samara sat on her new comfortable couch as she waited for Ondrej. Ten minutes later, the doorbell rang. Grabbing her waist-length black Shearling coat and pink clutch, she went to the door. Ondrej stood on the opposite side of the door looking dapper in black fitted jeans, a black turtleneck, and shiny black Calvin Klein dress shoes. A lone gold Cuban link chain hung from his neck, and he completed the ensemble with an opened black and white Herringbone pea coat.

"Okay, Mr. GQ, I see you!" Samara belted after she took a moment to drink him all in.

A small smirk appeared on his face as he said, "You are always being extra. You ready?"

"I am, Big Poppa. Let's go."

"Have you had anything to drink since earlier?"

"No. I am practically sober now," Samara said just as her shoe got caught in a crack in her driveway, causing her to stumble.

Ondrej quickly grabbed her arm to catch her but laughed all at the same time. He said: "Yeah, sure."

On the ride to the restaurant, they listened to music and held hands as if one or the other was going to fly out of the car at any moment. Ondrej and Samara reached *The Nest* at exactly nine o'clock and walked into the well-lit establishment. They were seated shortly after they arrived. Ondrej ordered a *Southern Screwdriver* for Samara, and a Heineken for himself.

"I don't ever bring females around Richie. He's a bit much to handle but I hope he keeps himself in check because he has a date," Ondrej said, taking a sip of his beer.

"I may be sweet and nice with you but believe me, I can hold my own. But if he has that type of energy, he better not want to go there with me." Samara was in a good mood and didn't want nothing to fuck it up. She had a new house, a new man, and a new lease of life.

"I know you could hold your own. I don't doubt that. But I'm telling you from experience, he could be loud, obnoxious, and he speaks his mind, no matter how hurtful it is."

"He's your friend. I'm sure that even through those things we will get along." Samara was remaining hopeful. However, this was Dre's best friend. Richie and his date walked in. Samara was shocked that Richie was a white boy. A good looking one too and if she was into white boys, Richie definitely would have had a chance with her. Richie was dressed down in all black too, but instead had on butter constructions and a black pea coat. His date was a pretty female; she had rich chocolate colored skin, chinky eyes, a small button nose, and medium-full lips. She was wearing Burberry printed pants, a cream colored sweater, black pumps, and a Burberry cropped puffer coat. *'Okay, Miss Girl can dress,'* Samara thought to herself.

When Richie and his date got closer to the table, Dre's jaw tightened, causing Samara to look on in confusion. Dre and Richie slapped each other up but Ondrej's face was set in a grimace at the woman. Ondrej's eyes softened when he turned his attention to Samara. He said, "Samara, this is my right hand—Richie. Richie, this is my lady—Samara."

"What's up?" Richie said while reaching his hand out to shake Samara's hand.

"Hey," Samara responded and took Richie's hand into hers.

"Since these two motherfuckers are rude and not going to introduce me, my name is Destiny but everybody calls me Des," Richie's date said as she reached her hand out to shake Samara's hand.

100

"Umm, hey," Samara innocently said and waved instead of taking her hand. Samara could feel the tension coming off of Ondrej, so why would she even play in his face like that. Destiny took her hand back and grilled Samara.

"Richie, what is she doing here?" Dre asked.

"I should have given you a heads-up but my original date canceled on me at the last minute. Destiny didn't have anything to do, so I invited her out."

Ondrej only had to look up at Richie for him to understand that he fucked up. Everybody took their seats and ordered drinks and food. After two hours of shots, the tension was gone and the fun had started. Samara didn't know what was going on, but she was glad that the vibe changed. They spent almost three hours at *The Nest* before Ondrej decided that it was time to leave. Samara watched Ondrej dap up Richie, and she couldn't help but think negatively about Richie. There was something about him that turned her off. As soon as she got a chance to, she was going to let Ondrej know.

When they exited the restaurant, they headed in the direction to where they parked the car, while Richie and Destiny walked in the other direction. The temperature dropped significantly and they began to speed walk to the car. When inside of the car, Ondrej turned it on and waited for it to warm up.

"Are you ready to decorate the tree?" Ondrej asked as he pulled off from the curb.

"Man, listen. That tree might have to wait until tomorrow." Samara laughed.

"Nah, we getting it done tonight. Christmas as a kid was my favorite holiday. I have to admit the past few years, I haven't been much up to celebrating. Since I lost my sisters to the system actually. This may sound corny but spending Christmas with you feels like there is some type of normalcy in my life. I already know you don't have to go to work until noon tomorrow. Don't be a party pooper."

Samara didn't dare deny him this. If this would put him in good spirits, then she was down. She smiled and said, "Okay, let's go decorate a tree."

Surprised that she agreed, he grabbed her hand into his and continued on to her house. Samara was proving that she wasn't like the other women and it was happening fast. So fast his head was spinning. As soon as they made it to Samara's house, they left the warmth of the car and ran into the house.

"I will never get used to this cold weather. Ain't no way in hell it needs to be this cold," Samara said as they took their shoes off at the door.

"You just got to dress warmer."

Samara side eyed him. She said, "Beauty costs and if I have to deal with a little bit of cold weather to look this cute then so be it."

Ondrej shook his head, not understanding her logic. He said, "Women. Let's go decorate this tree."

Samara decided to put the tree in the window that faced the front of the house. The tree looked pretty damn real for it to be fake. They placed red and gold garland around the tree before they began hanging the red and gold ornaments. Samara thought this would be a good time to ask about the exchange at the restaurant.

"First, let me say that if I am being nosey, feel free to tell me to mind my business. What was the animosity with Destiny at the restaurant?" Samara asked.

Ondrej knew that Samara would ask about it. He was at least hoping that she waited until another day. He knew there was a chance that his mood would change and Ondrej was in a good mood. He placed his hand onto the tree and took a seat on the couch.

"Destiny is, well, was one of my best friend's wife. He recently passed and I feel like she is being sneaky about something. I explained this to Richie and he assured me that he would get to the bottom of things. Him knowing that I wasn't fucking with her like that, he should've known not to bring that woman around me. Then I figured that the reason why he brought her could very well be him doing exactly what he said he was going to do. I put my feelings to the side because I owed it to Leon to find out the truth." It was Ondrej's guilt eating away at him. Knowing that he should have done his own investigating into the manner. There was sadness in his voice that wasn't there a minute and a half ago.

"Thank you for sharing that. I think now is the time to tell you that there is something about Richie that I don't trust. It could be the shiftiness in his eyes but I do not trust that man!" Samara confessed as she crossed her legs at the ankle and wrapped her arms around her knees.

"You just met him."

"I know. Which is why it is concerning."

Ondrej's mood was changing and he wanted to change the subject, but before he did, he was going to defend his friend. He said, "Richie is a lot of things but sneaky or shifty isn't one of them. I've known him my whole life and he is more than my best friend. He is my brother and if I had to choose somebody to save my life, it would be him."

"Ondrej, all I'm saying is to keep what I said in the back of your mind."

"I don't need to. You don't have to trust him. He's my friend and I do. Now if it's okay with you, I would like to change the topic and finish decorating the tree."

"That's fine by me," Samara agreed. She didn't want to get into an argument or disagreement with him. She just wanted to let him know that that is where she stood with Richie. Silence enveloped the house as they continued to decorate the tree.

When they were done, Ondrej wrapped his arms around Samara, taking her into a hug. He placed a kiss on her forehead, then her nose, and lastly her lips. His hands slid down her back and then cupped her ass into his hands.

"I'm sorry for being aggressive with the things I said. As you can see, I am overprotective over the ones that I love. I will take how you feel about Richie into consideration and I will do my best to not have him around you." Ondrej was sorry about how he came at her. But he was overprotective over Richie, and his first instinct was to always protect him. He meant what he said about Richie being his brother. He was for sure his brother's keeper.

"I get it. You don't have to apologize because I would have popped off the same way and probably would have tried to fight you," Samara replied with a soft chuckle. She wanted to lighten the mood.

Ondrej ducked down just a bit to place a kiss on Samara's lips. She closed her eyes and opened her mouth, receiving his tongue into her warm mouth. Ondrej's hands went to the back of her neck and caressed it with the tips of his fingers. The kiss was sensual at first but soon turned to hunger. Their hands couldn't keep still. They tore into each other with such ferocity, it was like two lions in the jungle fighting. Samara found herself on the couch naked, while Ondrej stood in front of her, looking every bit of an African god. His body looked very delectable, and Samara was waiting there with her plate and fork, ready to eat him up. His body was toned with the right amount of muscle with a tad bit of fat. He was on the beginning side of being stocky. Samara felt like she was in a movie. The part where it moves in slow motion before they fuck, yeah that part! She looked up at him while he stood over her with a smirk on his face. He was slowly stroking himself. Samara was in shock at how he grew with each stroke. Ondrej was a good seven inches by the time he stopped stroking because of Samara pulling him closer.

Samara stuck her tongue out, holding his meat with her left hand. She licked the tip and around his head before she took his head in her mouth. Looking up at Ondrej, she slowly moved her head down the shaft of his penis until he fit snugly in her throat. Ondrej's mouth hung open as he watched her swallow him up, her lips touching his stubble of pubic hair he was sporting.

In a flash, Samara was moving her head back and forth, the head of his dick hitting her tonsils. Pausing just for a second, she spit on the tips of her fingers, and began to massage his balls. Her tongue felt like velvet on the under part of his shaft. As if his dick wasn't wet enough, Samara pulled him from her mouth and let spit drip onto his dick. Samara leaned in a little further down and placed his balls into her mouth. She beat his dick while she sucked and hummed on his sack. *She sucks dick like a porn star,* Ondrej thought. She was back on his dick with her mouth, switching her rhythm every thirty seconds. Ondrej felt himself just about to drop his kids off at the playground, or—in other words—her throat, but he had to sample what she had between her legs before he allowed himself to cum off her head alone. Ondrej pulled away from Samara, tripping over the ledge of the rug and falling onto the love seat.

"Yo, chill! Samara, what the fuck!" Ondrej yelled. He was breathless after what Samara just did to him. She looked at him with a smirk of amusement on her face.

"What?" she asked innocently.

He grilled her playfully before he replied, "You know exactly what. Don't sit there and play like you don't know what I'm talking about."

"I didn't even do anything."

Ondrej wasn't about to play with Samara. He was about to teach her a lesson. Without another word, Dre grabbed Samara's body without clothes on. The image will remain etched in his mind for the rest of his life. Since he never went upstairs, he allowed for Samara to walk up first and enjoyed the view of her ass cheeks bouncing in his face. When they got up the stairs, Samara continued to walk down a long hallway until she reached her bedroom. She gave Ondrej a show as she cat walked on her tiptoes to her bed. When Samara got to the foot of the bed, she bent over at the waist and laid her chest flat onto the bed. Ondrej stood at the door, slowly stroking himself. *She could play all she wanted to. I'm about to show her ass who the fucking boss is,* Ondrej thought.

Samara climbed onto the bed seductively and got into the doggy style position. She sucked on her fingers for a moment and then reached back to slide her fingers up and down her slit. She was teasing him and he enjoyed it. Samara removed her fingers from her sticky pot, placed her fingers in her mouth, and licked them clean. Her ass jiggled as she slightly twerked her ass cheeks one at a time. Samara reached around and held a magnum condom between her fingers. Ondrej was harder than a brick as he made his way to the bed. He stood behind Samara as he took the condom from her and proceeded to put it on.

"You like to play, I see?" Ondrej questioned while rolling the condom onto his dick. Samara giggled until Ondrej firmly smacked her right ass cheek. Dre slid his index finger between her slit, flickering his finger over her clit. Squatting down, Ondrej removed his finger and replaced it with his tongue. Samara didn't expect for him to eat her pussy from the back. His hands gripped her ass cheeks as he rocked her back and forth on his tongue. Dre didn't go down on all of the females he had been with. At least he didn't with the women that he was just fucking to fulfill his sexual needs. But he knew that Samara was his lady before they had gotten to this point.

"Mmm, right there, Dre!" Samara purred when she felt him hit her spot. He was lapping up every bit of her, almost daring her to cum all over his face. Samara's legs shook, and her muscles in her lower abdomen tightened as she moaned out her orgasm. This went on for another five minutes before Samara tapped out.

"Samara zero, Dre one." Ondrej chuckled as he climbed into bed. Samara rolled onto her back and spread her legs for Ondrej to climb in between.

"Oh, so we keeping count?" Samara questioned with a smirk on her face.

Ondrej didn't answer. He simply placed his lips on hers. Ondrej got comfortable on his knees, with Samara's legs on either side of his waist. Sliding into her felt like heaven. The way her muscles tightened around him let Ondrej know that this was his new home. Ondrej couldn't help himself. He had to sit in it for a minute because if he moved, he was liable to cum without getting in at least ten strokes.

It felt like he was in it forever, but it was actually just a few moments. Slowly, he began to move in and out of Samara. Her hands wrapped around the back of his neck and interlocked as she matched his rhythm with her hips.

"Damn, this shit is good," Ondrej whispered in Samara's ear. She thanked him with a flick of her tongue to his ear. Ondrej ducked his head down, taking one of her nipples into his mouth. He remembered the stunt that she pulled in the living room; he pulled out and told her to get back into doggy style. Samara did what she was told while Ondrej positioned himself on the balls of his feet. Once Ondrej was in her good enough, he pounded away in her pussy. Her juices coated his length, and her moans drove him insane while he watched her ass move in waves as he slammed into her. Ondrej could no longer hold onto his nut. He slid out of Samara before she was able to cum again, laid on his back, and told her to climb on top. With no hesitation, Samara planted her feet flat on either side of his body, her back to him, and bounced up and down, almost instantly bringing both of them to climax.

"Fuckkkk!" Ondrej grunted as he spilled his seeds into the condom. Samara followed soon after. She remained on top of him while she caught her breath, and his meat shrunk back to its soft state. Samara didn't know it yet, but at that moment, she had fallen in love.

Mimi

Chapter Nine

Christmas, New Year, and Valentine's Day had come and gone, and spring was finally showing its head. Samara was floating on cloud nine. She recently just came back from a trip to Hawaii with Ondrej. He was under a lot of stress with his organization, and he suggested they take a short vacation. They had only been gone for four nights, but for the both of them, it was the best four days of their lives. Samara felt like a new woman, and the glow on her face told it all. Her boutiques were booming and for the meantime, it felt like her life was finally going right.

Samara was spending her lunch hour at a cute little diner near her shop. She left Amber and a few girls in charge. She was meeting Helen, per her request. Samara spotted Helen as soon as she walked in. With a smile on her face, she walked over to Helen and greeted her with a tight hug.

"My, my, my, aren't we glowing today? What got you glowing like that? It's been so long since I've seen this on you!" Helen said. Whatever it was, Helen liked it for Samara.

"Life, Helen. I'm just happy."

"Does this life have a penis and some balls?" Helen asked, looking over her coffee mug as she took a sip of liquid goodness.

"Helen!" Samara fell into a fit of laughter.

"Being on this earth for sixty-plus years, I know some things. It's either a man or a baby and I know it's not a baby. Who is he?"

Samara went back and forth with herself. She wanted to tell Helen about Ondrej, but it was still early and she didn't want to jinx anything. Samara explained, "I'm just happy, Helen. My boutiques are doing well. I just came back from Hawaii, so maybe it could be my tan."

"Play innocent all you want to. I know otherwise. You don't have to say anything now but eventually I want to meet him." Helen spoke with a smile on her face.

As much as Samara didn't want to admit anything, she agreed with allowing Helen to meet Ondrej. The waitress came and took their order of home fried bacon, scrambled eggs with cheese, and

French toast. Samara and Helen made small talk while they waited for the food to come out. It was at Helen's request that they met. From Helen's body language, Samara knew that she was nervous. It was making Samara antsy and the fear struck her. *What if something happened to Ryan?* Samara thought in panic. When the waitress brought their food out, Helen dug in while Samara stewed in fear as her stomach twisted in knots.

"Samara, are you okay? Why aren't you eating?" Helen asked when she noticed that she was the only one eating.

"You were the one who wanted me to meet you and I didn't think anything about it. But your body language is screaming that something is wrong. Is it Ryan? Is he okay?" Samara asked, trying her best to keep her tears in check.

"Look at you still caring for that man. Ryan is okay. I didn't want to talk about him. It's about me. But I was hoping that what I wanted to talk about could wait until we were done eating." Helen wiped her mouth with her napkin, placed it on the table, and sat back against the cushioned booth.

Samara was confused. Was Helen and Paul having marital issues and Helen needed advice? Samara took a sip of her coffee before she spoke. She asked, "What's wrong? Are you and Paul okay?"

"Yes, we are fine. This is hard for me to say but let me just say this. Whether you and Ryan are together or not, I still consider you to be my daughter. So if there is something that is going on with me that he has to know about, then you will too."

Samara interrupted Helen in panic, she asked, "What's wrong?"

"If you stop interrupting me, I will get to my point. Are you done with all of your questions?"

"Yes," Samara replied, animating that she was going to keep her lips zipped.

"This is hard enough, let me just get it out. I was recently diagnosed with stage three ovarian cancer. Now before you lose your shit, my doctor has a plan for aggressive treatment and it's going to work, and I will be fine."

"That's all you wanted to say? You got to give me a little more than that Helen. If you were going to be nonchalant, you could have given me a call."

Helen should have known she couldn't just slide past this. Helen had spent years upon years bottling up her emotions so much that she doesn't know any other way to deal with them. She taught herself to suck it up and do what needed to be done. Her vision was like a tunnel when it came to her emotions.

"I am fucking scared, Samara." Helen spoke just above a whisper. Samara immediately took Helen's hands into hers and squeezed them. Almost immediately, the tears poured from Helen's eyes. Samara let Helen's hands go and moved into her side of the booth next to Helen and wrapped her arms around her. Helen's body shook as she sobbed uncontrollably.

"Listen, Helen, there is no need to be scared. Stage three ovarian cancer is still curable. You have a strong support team, especially me. If you need anything at any time of the day, don't hesitate to call me." The tears were fresh in Samara's eyes. There was nothing Samara could say to make Helen feel better. She sat and hugged Helen until she began to wipe her eyes.

"I have been a bitch my entire life because I was raised in an environment that told me that in order to be a real woman, you didn't take shit from nobody. Over the years I have been a bitch for reasons and others not so much. My biggest regret though is how I treated you. I had no reason to do so. I never gave you a chance until I got caught and was forced into it." Helen paused to chuckle at her statement. Samara joined in too because they had come a long way. Helen continued, "Paul and I hit a rough patch. He wasn't as sexual as I was and I sought pleasure elsewhere. I swear after that day, I never did that shit again."

Remembering that day caused Samara to chuckle. Without knowing it, she basically forced Helen to like her and the outcome was good. Helen adored Samara and wished that she would have gotten to know Samara sooner. Once Helen's tears were all dried up, Samara moved back over to her side of the booth.

"Helen, if you ever need me in any way, please don't hesitate to call me. I don't care what time it is, just please make sure you do. You are not in this alone!" Samara stated sincerely.

"Thank you. I have an appointment for my first round of chemo in two weeks. Paul and Ryan said that they will assist me. However, if you have some time away from your new man, I would like it if you were to accompany me."

Samara playfully rolled her eyes and replied, "Just let me know what day, the time, and place. Text me the info later. Let's eat 'cause now that my anxiety is gone, my stomach is screaming to feed it."

"Shit! Mine is almost done." Helen laughed.

She scooped some eggs into her mouth. Samara's thoughts remained on swim even after their conversation. Ryan was an only child, and she knew how close he was to his mom so it melted her heart at the thoughts of the pain he must be going through. She made a mental note to send Ryan a text just to make sure he was holding up. For the remainder of their meal, they made small talk and Helen continued to hint to Samara, who expertly dodged her attempts and changed the subject each chance she got.

Later On, In the Evening

Samara completed her day at the boutique after her brunch with Helen. She found herself thinking on and off about Helen. She knew there was nothing that she could do, but she couldn't help but feel helpless. When Samara got back to work, she unblocked Ryan to ask how he was holding up. He replied that he was surprisingly taking the news well and he was confident that his mother would heal fully and beat cancer's ass. Samara ended the text message by giving Ryan her condolences. She placed Ryan back on her block list when he started talking crazy nonsense about them meeting to have a conversation. She was good on that.

Amber was hosting a booze and food ordeal at her house for Samara, Samirah, Sheeka, and herself. She was making tacos, mixing sangria, and pouring shots of Jose Cuervo. Samara was running late but she wanted to stop at her house to shower and change. She was working her ass off and worked up a sweat throughout the day, and she felt disgusted as her clothes clung to her body.

When she approached her driveway, she quickly parked and ran inside to take a shower. She was in and out of her house in forty minutes, and on her way to Amber's house. Amber only lived ten minutes away from Samara, which was a blessing. Samara noticed that everyone was already there, judging by her sister and Sheeka's car in the driveway. Knowing that the door was unlocked, she walked inside once she was sure her car doors were locked.

"It's about motherfucking time that you got your ass here. What were you doing? Fucking that fine ass man you got!" Sheeka shouted. Samara automatically knew that Sheeka was half past tipsy and wasn't up for Sheeka's shenanigans.

"Don't worry about what me and my man do. Who the hell let this bitch start drinking before I got here?" Samara asked with annoyance.

"She was lit when she got here. What took you so long to get here?" Samirah asked, handing Samara a glass of sangria.

"Y'all know I like to have a good time. No harm, no foul. Samara, don't take shit to heart. I be just fucking with you."

"Sheeka, I'm not hardly paying you any mind but you for real need to stop drinking and driving. You can hurt yourself or someone else!" Samara lectured. She didn't care about Sheeka's drinking; it was her actions that irked Samara.

Amber joined them in the living room with a tray displaying an array of tacos. There was chicken, fish, and birria. Amber placed the tray on the coffee table, as everyone took seats around the table. Amber spoke, "Y'all bitches better be grateful that I was in the mood for drinks and tacos. There are more tacos in the kitchen. These are just to get something on our stomachs. I'm going to go change real quick, so eat and drink up, bitches."

Samara didn't hesitate to grab one of the shredded chicken tacos. She hadn't eaten since lunch with Helen. Before she knew it, Samara was grabbing another taco.

"Guess who I saw today?" Sheeka sang out with a smirk on her face.

"Who?" Samirah asked while finishing her last bite of a fish taco.

Sheeka walked closer to Samara and said, "Ryan fine ass."

"Why every time you talk about Ondrej or Ryan, you mention that they are fine. Ain't nothing fine about Ryan trifling ass!" Samirah smacked. However, Samirah wasn't the only one who noticed. Samara did too and it wasn't just with Ryan and Ondrej.

"I can't say a man is fine?" Sheeka slurred.

"Yeah, you can, but when you constantly say it about Samara's dudes, it gets sus, sis. That's your friend. Nothing about Ryan or Ondrej should be fine to you!" Samirah replied angrily.

Samara interrupted because she knew that it was going to go left pretty soon. After lunch with Helen, all she wanted to do was enjoy a drama-free night with her girls. She said, "Samirah, just drop it. I had a long day and Sheeka just drunk, talking out the side of her neck."

Samirah eyed her sister to let her know that she will bring it up at a later time when it's just them. Samirah sucked her teeth and grabbed her cup to get a refill. Amber had walked back into the room, ready to turn up until she noticed the grim looks on everybody's face.

"Aww, hell. What the hell happened?" Amber asked.

"I'm going to the bathroom," Sheeka replied and switched her ass to the bathroom.

"That woman is impossible," Samirah hissed as she came back with a glass of something dark.

"What happened?" Amber asked, confused.

"We can talk about it later. Let's enjoy the night. Besides, I got some fucked up news that I have to share with y'all."

Sheeka came back into the living room and took a seat on the chaise lounge without another peep from her. Amber got herself a drink and sat down on the floor. Everybody was all ears, and eyes were on Samara.

"Helen asked me out to lunch today. I thought we were going to catch up but she told me that she has stage three ovarian cancer.

And I feel hella guilty all those times I wished death on her!" Samara cried out. Their past was troublesome, and Samara knew it was wrong but at the time she wished it she didn't care.

Amber stood up and took a seat next to Samara. She used her hand to rub Samara's back. She said, "I'm sorry to hear that and you have nothing to feel guilty about. Helen was a bitch to you for no reason and those were your feelings at the time. You could now only ask for forgiveness and be a part of her support team."

"What if God doesn't forgive me?" Samara sniffled.

"He forgives all, Samara, and you know that. You and Helen are in a different space right now and that's all that matters." Samirah confirmed. The room grew quiet as Amber and Samirah comforted Samara.

"Ain't she too old to have ovarian cancer? Shouldn't her eggs and shit be dried up or something?" Sheeka callously asked. The room grew quiet as all eyes turned to Sheeka. Samirah was too through with Sheeka. She picked up her phone and opened the Lyft app.

"Give me your keys," Samirah stated as she stood over Sheeka. Sheeka looked up at Samirah with confusion.

"For what?" Sheeka asked.

"Give me your keys!" Samirah was growing impatient. Sheeka's mouth was going to write herself a check her ass can't cash. Samirah's face told Sheeka that she was serious. Without further hesitation Sheeka handed over her keys.

"Why do you need my keys though?"

"Your ride is going to be here in five minutes."

"My ride? What do you mean by ride? I'm not ready to go."

"You may not be ready to go but your mouth is saying otherwise. Your friend is going through a lot, but you can't even comprehend to console her. You need to go home and sleep that shit off and I am not letting you drive."

Sheeka jumped up and tried to grab her keys from Samirah. Who was Samirah to make this decision for her? Samara jumped up to stop the two before they began to tussle.

"Sheeka, your mouth is going to get you into a lot of trouble. Just go home for the night, sleep it off and I will see you tomorrow. I know it's the alcohol talking for you which is why I am not letting what you say get to me. If your drinking is going to be a problem then you seriously need to get some help!" Samara stated. In Sheeka's inebriated mind, she felt like Samara and Samirah were attacking her.

"Amber, you're not going to say anything?" Sheeka asked, looking for Amber's help.

"What you want me to say, Sheeka? They are not wrong. What you said was fucked up and apparently you said something while I wasn't in the room. All we are asking is that you sleep on it."

When Sheeka realized that they were all against her, she grabbed her things and stood in front of Amber's house to wait for her Lyft. She was fuming and by the end of the night they were going to get told about themselves. Back in the house, Samara, Samirah, and Amber continued their night of booze and food. Samara needed a drink more than ever. She was sad for her friend and hoped like hell that Sheeka heard them and would straighten her shit up.

Chapter Ten

Back in the Day

Water droplets dropped down the drain from the bathroom sink as the sun slowly made its way up into the sky on a hot July morning. Sweat covered Ondrej's body, and the plastic that covered his mattress stuck to his body, as if it was a second skin. The fan in the room was useless; it was only circulating the humid air, causing Ondrej to open his eyes in frustration. There was a heat wave in Brooklyn for the past week, and he'd barely gotten any sleep. Blinking his eyes a few times, he sighed and sat up on his bed, aiming the fan directly into his face. Surprisingly, it worked just enough to calm his frustrated attitude.

It wasn't even eight in the morning, and Ondrej decided to get up and get ready for his day. He was fourteen and he planned on spending his day at one of his friend's houses that had air conditioning. While there was a heat wave, it had felt better outside than it did in the house, but he suffered long enough and he planned on convincing one of his boys to stay in.

Ondrej made his way to the bathroom, grateful that he was able to enjoy a nice cool shower without being bombarded. He was the oldest of four, and sharing the bathroom with his siblings and mother was always a task in itself. He was the only boy, and getting in the bathroom before his sisters was always a blessing. Ondrej brushed his teeth and hopped into the shower, enjoying the cool water.

Knock! Knock! Knock!

"Ondrej, come on, I gotta pee!" his youngest sister, Damani, yelled through the door. Damani was the youngest between her and her twin sister Kamani, but she acted like she was the boss of all of them.

"A'ight, damn. I'm coming out!" he responded. Rinsing the soap from his body, he cut the water off, grabbed his towel and wrapped it around his waist. Damani was in front of the door, hopping from one foot to the next, trying not to pee on herself. Ondrej chuckled and made his way inside his room to get dressed.

After his shower, he cooled off significantly but he knew this wasn't going to last long. Moments after he was dressed, there was a knock on the door and without waiting for an answer, in walked his twelve-year-old sister Ishani.

"You need to learn how to wait for an answer before you just walk into somebody's room." Ondrej huffed.

"Oh, please. I heard you when you got out of the shower and I gave you enough time to get dressed." Ishani took a seat on her brother's bed.

"What do you want?" Ondrej asked. His sisters, just like anybody else's, were annoying, but he loved them to the ends of the earth. None of them had the same father of course except for the twins, but none of their fathers were ever around. Their mother, Tootie, was a prostitute when she had gotten pregnant with each of them. Their fathers were her pimps and as soon as they found out that she was pregnant, they would throw her to the curb to fend for herself. When Tootie was pregnant with Ondrej, she stopped prostituting long enough to get help from welfare and get an apartment. When her life began to take a turn for the better, she met Ishani's father. For Tootie, it was love at first sight, but when she got pregnant again, he ran off on her. He pimped her out enough to blame her for getting pregnant by a trick, never thinking of getting a DNA test.

By the time Tootie got pregnant with the twins, she had given up on everything. The job she had at McDonalds since Ondrej was two, she stopped going to. Instead of attempting to find another job, she allowed welfare to take care of her rent. Welfare also gave her food and cash assistance. She had to show up every other week for appointments and complete a certain number of hours of office work in order to get the little bit of cash they gave her.

The twins' father was the worst. He was a low-down crackhead but had a stable of bitches that was working the track for him, making him money to feed his addiction. Tootie quickly became his bottom bitch and proved that she would do anything he asked of her, including smoking crack while she was pregnant with the twins.

"Mama ain't answering her door, and me and the twins are hungry." Ishani pouted.

"What you mean? There should still be food in there."

"Dre, I checked. There's a few frozen tins of meat in there but no breakfast or lunch."

Ondrej's face twisted up. He knew that there was more food because he made sure that he got enough to last two weeks. Ondrej was taking care of the household as if he was the head of household. His mother was no longer capable of doing so. She relied on the glass dick too much to bother to take care of her kids. Tootie would hide the food stamp card and use that to get crack, so it was always up to Ondrej to step up to the plate. He stole anything that he could get his hands on. He even would rob low level hustlers in different neighborhoods in order to get the money to feed his sisters, and to make sure that the house and their clothes were cleaned.

"Where the fuck is everything?" He growled. This was a reason why he disliked his mother. He marched from the kitchen to her room door that was at the end of the long hallway. Trying the door knob, he wiggled it to open it and it didn't budge. He began to yell her name and bang on the door, causing his sister to look on. This was nothing new.

"What?" Tootie yelled, swinging the door open.

"Where the hell is all the food that I put in here for the girls?"

"What food? I'm barely home so how am I supposed to know?"

Ondrej looked at his mother and knew she was lying. She did this all of the time and used the same damn excuse of her not being home. Ondrej's patience was wearing thin. Dre looked back at his sisters and then to his mother. He said, "You do this all the time. I risk going to jail every few weeks so I could feed them and you end up selling the shit for some crack! What kind of mother does that?"

"You ain't too old to get your ass whooped, boy! Who do you think you are talking to? You better go on and take that shit somewhere else."

"I ain't the only one that needs their ass whooped. I'm putting food in the house for them again and if it goes missing, you're going to have a problem."

Mimi

Ondrej walked out of the door with his mother calling him every name under the sun except for a child of God. His anger built up. He didn't want to be an angry teenager, but being forced to provide for his sisters and not enjoy his teen years, he had every right to be angry.

As Ondrej made his way down the pissy smelling staircase in his building, his mind scrambled trying to figure out a way he was going to get his sisters food to eat for the next few days. This was not in his plans, but he had to do what he had to do in order to provide for his sisters. The streets were quiet but he knew this was only temporary. Ondrej walked up the pathway towards Dwight Street. He was walking in the direction of his best friend Richie's house.

Upon reaching his house, he knocked on the door loud enough to hope that only Richie heard it. Richie's mom—Ms. Lisa—worked overnight at Long Island College Hospital as a registered nurse. Ondrej knew she had only arrived an hour prior to his arrival and didn't want to wake her if she was asleep. Ondrej was just about to give up and walk away when he heard the locks being undone. Ms. Lisa was on the opposite side holding her robe closed.

"Ondrej, what are you doing here so early?" she asked, placing her hands on her hips. Ms. Lisa was too thick to be a white woman. Richie didn't like it too much because his friends would always tease him and say that they would have her bent over somewhere.

"Oh, I'm sorry for waking you, Ms. Lisa, but I needed to speak with Richie right quick," Ondrej said, trying his hardest to keep his eyes on hers.

"It's almost eight in the morning. You know he isn't awake." Ms. Lisa raised her eyebrow and looked at him. She continued, "In fact, the only time you are here this early is if your mother did something to piss you off. What she do now?"

Ms. Lisa moved to the side and let Ondrej in. He sat at the kitchen table and exhaled. He didn't realize that what his mother had done made him tense. Ms. Lisa pulled a chair out and took a seat herself.

"My mother took almost a week's worth of food and sold it," he admitted and dropped his head. Ms. Lisa rolled her eyes because she's heard this story plenty of times through her son. The horror that Ondrej and his sisters had to endure, she couldn't fathom. Ms. Lisa got up from her seat and grabbed her purse. Going inside, she handed him sixty dollars.

"Here. This isn't much but it will do. I trust that you know how to shop and make this stretch. I'm sorry y'all have to deal with this."

"I'm going to figure out a better way."

"You shouldn't have to, Ondrej. You're fourteen and you should enjoy being a child."

"I know, Ms. Lisa, but there is no other way. We don't know our fathers and my mother ain't worth nothing. I'm going to make sure my sisters will always be good no matter what. I'm honestly all they have and I have to show and prove."

Ms. Lisa smiled at Ondrej's words and leaned over to pat him on his head. She hated that Ondrej was such a good kid being forced into such a horrible life. She would pray that the streets didn't gobble him and his sisters up. Ondrej thanked Ms. Lisa and made his way to the grocery store hoping his mother didn't touch this food.

***

Ondrej managed to get enough food to last them for a week. He couldn't carry all of the bags by himself, so he borrowed the shopping cart from the store. By this time, people were finally making their way outside to enjoy the mugginess of the heatwave, and all Ondrej wanted to do was take another shower. He made it to his building and grabbed all of the shopping bags just so he wouldn't have to make another trip. He even placed two or three bags over his head so they dangled from his neck.

Three flights later, he was winded and soaked in sweat. Placing the bags on the floor, he heard glass shattering and females screaming. He realized that it was coming from his apartment. Leaving the grocery bags in the hallway, he raced to the door and stormed in. The sight before his eyes almost made him throw up. His twin sisters were huddled in the corner, holding their hands over their ears screaming for help. Ishani was on the floor with a strange man lying on top of her, holding her hands down with one of his while holding his dick in his other hand. Ishani was trying her hardest to keep her legs closed, but he was stronger than her.

Coming back to his senses, Ondrej ran over to his sister, kicked the man in his face, and yelled, "Get the fuck off my sister!"

Ishani dragged herself from under the man and got away as fast as she could. Recouping from the kick to the face, the man stood to his feet and glared at Ondrej. His sisters screamed for their mother as this strange man charged towards Ondrej. Ondrej swung but missed as the man ducked and grabbed Ondrej by his legs. Before Ondrej knew it, he was in the air and the next he was on his back with the wooden coffee table shattered around him. The door to the apartment opened and the people who heard the commotion were gathered at the door watching.

Tootie, their mother, came out of her room, her eyes bulged out of her head and her jaw rocking from side to side. The strange man was standing over Ondrej with his foot hanging over his head. The girls continued to scream and cry as Ondrej saw the boot coming down to his face. Suddenly, the strange man went flying across the room. Ondrej got up from the floor as he watched another strange man pummel the first strange man. Ondrej turned his attention to his mother, and in that moment he wanted to put his hands on her.

"What the fuck were you doing while this man was trying to rape my sister!" Ondrej yelled.

"I-I just was in-in—" Her mouth twitched.

"You were just in there smoking crack! How dare you! You ain't no mother to us!"

As Ondrej spewed curses to his mother, darkness clouded her eyes as she said, "It was time that young whore began to spread her legs. There's bills and things that need to be paid."

Fire danced in Ondrej's eyes as he tried to process what he just heard his mother say. In his calmest tone, he asked, "What did you say?"

"Ayo, Shine, we got to go. One time on their way!" a light-skinned man with a baby face said, coming inside of the apartment. Shine got off of the rapist and got ready to leave the apartment. He saw the look on Ondrej's face and walked up to him.

"It's not worth it. But if you need anything, come look for me. Niggas know Shine." With that, he was gone. Police filed inside of the apartment and began to conduct their questioning. That was the last day that he saw his sisters and the day he began to hate the woman who gave birth to him.

Present Day

Ondrej had been up since four in the morning due to the nightmare that he had. Every few weeks he would have nightmares from his childhood trauma. The most prevalent one is the one where he last saw his sisters. Their innocent faces the day they were dragged out of that apartment will forever be ingrained in Ondrej's brain. He felt like he was at a point where he was supposed to protect them, but all he did was fail. He had no idea where to begin to look for them. He tried everything down to social media, and he still hadn't had any luck. It ate Ondrej up every single day that he didn't know where they were. Tears welled up in Ondrej's eyes as he sipped from a glass that was filled with Jack Daniels, a blunt burning between his fingers.

Ondrej thought about where he was in life. His organization was bringing in money hand over fist, he drove a nice car, had a nice house, and he had a woman that he thought he could spend the rest of his life with. But he would give all that up if it meant that he would have his sisters back. Some would think that his life was complete, but he lived with the guilt that he didn't protect his sisters every day, and every day he felt like a failure. He needed to find his sisters.

The sound of Samara's heels clicking across his hardwood floors alerted him, and he quickly wiped his face and straightened himself up. Samara appeared at the door of his office in a powder blue pantsuit, a white blouse and white pumps. Her hair was swopped into a low bun, and pearls adorned her neck and ears.

"Where the hell are you going looking presidential?" Ondrej asked with a chuckle.

Samara laughed and said, "I told you last night I had to be at the boutique that is on Jay Street today. I'm going to be there all day."

"Oh, yeah. I'm sorry, babes, you did," he responded as he sipped from his cup.

"Is everything okay?" Samara asked as she nervously smoothed out the invisible wrinkles that were in her suit. She never saw Ondrej drinking so early, and she knew that wasn't his first drink by the slight slur in his words.

"Everything is good. I just had some shit on my mind but everything is cool now. I gotta make some runs with Richie today in a few hours."

Samara walked over and placed a kiss on his lips. She stood up and said, "Sleep that liquor off. Make sure you are on point."

Ondrej smoothed his hands across her backside, squeezing one of her plump cheeks in his hand, and pulled his bottom lip between his teeth. He said, "If you are trying to make it to work on time, I suggest you leave now. I'm well on my way to being bricked up."

On any other day, she would take him up on his offer. She would have liked nothing more than to be bouncing on her man's dick and screaming his name against the walls. However, she had an important summer shipment coming that day and needed to be there. Samara looked at Ondrej's face, dragging her eyes across his facial features. *But his face would make a fantastic seat,* she thought to herself.

"It sounds tempting but we're gonna have to find a way to get in a little quickie. I gotta go before I make your face my seat." With a quick peck on the lips, Samara scurried out of the room to make sure that she made it to the store on time. With a grunt, Ondrej watched Samara's hips sway out of the room. That woman had a hold on him, and pretty soon he wouldn't be able to keep control of his dick every time he saw her. His attraction to Samara grew every day, just her smell alone could cause Ondrej to brick up. Ondrej relaxed his head against his chair, trying to will the throbbing in his dick to stop. Moments passed before Ondrej's eyes popped open and he grabbed his phone. He needed to release himself before he wound up with blue balls. Her scent still lingered while Ondrej searched for the perfect porno. When he found it, he pulled his dick out and went for broke.

Samara had time before she was to open the store, and she stopped to get breakfast. The line for the drive-thru at McDonald's was way too long, so she parked and went inside. When it was her turn, she ordered a chicken McGriddle, a hash brown, and orange juice. Her order took ten minutes, and she was rushing out the door to her shop. She made it with five minutes to spare, and she decided to eat her breakfast at the checkout counter. She placed her food at the counter and went to grab a rack of clothes she planned to put out and style her mannequins with.

An hour passed before Samara's stomach reminded her that she needed to eat. Running into her office, she placed her food in the microwave and waited for it to warm up. Just as she was making her way back to the counter, the door rang announcing people were entering.

"Good morning. Welcome to Sage. Feel free to look around and if you need any help just let me know." Samara spoke in a welcoming tone. The two women that entered smirked in Samara's direction and clutched their purses a little tighter. Soon as Samara peeped that shit, she knew that she was dealing with Karens. She would have played their game, but her food was more than important at that moment. She dug in while she sat and watched the two women.

"Where is good help when you need it?" the older of the two women said as they browsed the jewelry by the counter. The second woman laughed like something was funny.

"I told you to let me know if you needed help," Samara remarked while taking a sip from her orange juice.

"Well, it's pretty clear that eating is more important than helping customers. Obviously, you don't need anything more to eat."

Did this bitch just insinuate that I was fat? Oh hell no! Samara thought to herself. Samara wasn't fat but she did carry some weight in her ass, hips, and thighs. She was shaped like a woman, a black woman at that. She couldn't say so much for the stick bugs that stood in front of her.

"I'm gonna do whatever I want. I will eat, sleep, shit, and fuck in the middle of this room if I wanted to. If you wanted help, that's all you had to say."

"Oh my God! That's no way to speak to paying customers. I've shopped here for the past few months and I have never been treated this way! Where is your manager? The white woman who is always here."

Samara automatically knew that they were talking about Amber. Samara smirked at them. They were right. She was the manager and Samara was the boss. And last time she checked, the boss ran things.

"Oh, you mean Amber? Well, she's not in today so you got little ole me!" Samara rebutted in a sweet southern accent. She had the time today, and she wanted all the smoke.

"Well, we would like to speak to another manager," the younger one stated.

"Too bad there aren't any managers around. However, would you like to speak to the owner?"

The two Karens' eyes lit up like they hit big on a lottery ticket. They nodded simultaneously and said, "Yes, actually we would like that."

The smile on Samara's face grew wider she said, "Here she is. The looks on y'all faces told me all that I needed to know. Matter of fact, the comment about finding good help was what let me know what kind of people I was dealing with."

"Since you're the owner then you should know that eating on the sales floor is unprofessional. You people don't know how to be professional even if there was a handbook on it, and you shouldn't be allowed to have a business. You have no class and neither does this tired shop!" the older of the two said. She high-fived the younger one as if they were on to something by insulting Samara. Samara had something up her sleeve though. She's definitely going to get the last laugh.

"You people? Are you referring to black people? Karen and mini Karen, I don't know what era you are from but black people are entitled to the same things you cum-on-a-rag motherfuckers enjoy, but I'm preaching to the choir here. If you and every racist motherfucker took the time to learn history, you would know that people of the pasty color are genetic mutations of black people. But

Unbreak my Heart

I digress. The next time you want to be racist, remember that black people were here, on earth first, and know that we black people will always step on y'all necks. Now if you would please exit and shop elsewhere, I don't serve your kind. And by your kind, I don't mean the color of your skin. I mean racists like you two."

Karen and mini Karen's mouths dropped open, and they hastily walked towards the door. The door, however, didn't budge when they pushed on it. Samara held her stomach while she laughed deep from her belly. She had activated the door lock by one press of a button placed under the counter. She had it installed when she was just a few weeks shy from opening that location. She installed it from having boosters come in and steal her shit. The Karens looked at each other in confusion until they noticed Samara had stopped laughing and was now on the phone with 911. That's when they realized they were still holding several of Samara's items.

"She's lying!" they instantly yelled when they realized what was going on. Samara was instructed to stay on the phone with the dispatcher until the police arrived. When the police arrived, Samara unlocked the door for them, and the Karens immediately went into trying to use their white privilege. The police officers did their jobs and asked questions to figure out what happened. The two women still had the items in their hands when the police arrived. Samara was about being petty, and it meant calling the cops on these two women to teach them a lesson, but she wasn't petty enough to send them to jail. She snatched her items from their chicken feet looking fingers and banned them from shopping at either of her locations. In the future, if she opened another location, she would ban them from that one too. The whole fiasco lasted an hour and took too much energy from Samara.

By three o'clock, Samara had her summer shipment delivered. Between helping customers and thinking about her boo thang, Sheeka announced her presence by doing her infamous Brooklyn yell, *'Yerrrr!'* Samara was at the counter tagging her items and organizing them for her employees to place them on the sales floor.

"Why you always gotta be so damn loud?" Samara chuckled.

"Girl, you know I'm loud. What you doing?" Sheeka asked, peeking over the counter.

"What you about to help me with?"

"Dammit. I was hoping that you have at least been done with tagging before I got here. Every time I help you tag, I leave with bloody fingers!" Sheeka complained.

"You should have just learned to use the tag gun properly instead of being Billy Badass and just using it. Let's go, grab a gun, and let me tell you about this bullshit that I had to deal with this morning."

Sheeka did what Samara said as they fell into a conversation. It was like a breath of fresh air, as they laughed at the incident. Samara hated to change the subject but she wanted to speak with Sheeka about her behavior at Amber's apartment. Samara, although loving to turn up with Sheeka, knew there had to be something deeper going on with Sheeka.

"On a more serious note, Sheeka, is everything okay with you?" Samara asked with serious concern. As soon as Samara asked if she was okay, the floodgates opened up. Instantly, Samara wrapped her arms around Sheeka and rubbed her back. She reassured Sheeka that whatever it was, she was going to get through it and that everything was going to be okay.

After moments of Sheeka balling her eyes out, she had finally got herself together and was able to come out of her mouth. Congested, Sheeka said, "For the past six years I've been with the most amazing man that I have met. He took care of me, he was attentive, he was hood. Elijah was everything to me. He recently was killed, maybe four months ago, and I have yet to properly grieve Elijah. But he was married for ten years. I'd gotten pregnant by him four times and was forced to get an abortion the first three times. And I hated him for that. I was pregnant for the fourth time when he was killed. I was so stressed out that I miscarried. My hate for him grew even though he was gone. I recently went to the doctor's and was told that the abortions and miscarriage has damaged my uterus and I may never get the chance to have children. These are no excuses for my actions but if I had to admit, it played a part because I didn't know how to deal with it."

Samara couldn't even be mad that Sheeka had acted the way she did. She had a lot of shit going on and was dealing with it on her own. Samara was surprised that she was keeping it together the way that she was. *Shit! I would have cracked and cried to somebody.*

"Shit gonna be okay, Sheeka. Doctors know they shit but God got the final say, and you know that. Keep the faith and one day God will bless you with a baby. You got to meet him halfway though. The first thing you need to do is change your diet. When Samirah and Amber find out what's going on, they are gonna understand and be there for you."

Before Samara's last statement, Sheeka was just letting Samara ramble until Sheeka thought to herself. This is the conversation that she has been avoiding. Sheeka said, "That's just the thing, Samara—I don't know if I want to tell them."

Sheeka loved Samirah and Amber just as much as she loved Samara. However, Samara wasn't as judgemental as Samirah and Amber were. While Samirah and Samara were sisters and close, Sheeka noticed over the years that Samirah was closer to Amber than she was with Sheeka, and Sheeka noticed it while Samara had no clue.

Patting her friends eyes with Kleenex, Samara looked at Sheeka confused. She asked, "Why not? You know that they would understand and help you get through this. We are a sisterhood. And we help each other."

Sheeka loved the nurturing side of Samara, but that came with gullibility. Sheeka shook her head. As much as she wanted to believe Samara, she just knew that this was from the furthest of the truth. Sheeka said, "Samara, for the longest, I've noticed that I don't have the same support from Amber and Samirah that I get from you. If it's okay, I would like this to stay between us. Okay?"

"Yes, of course. I understand."

At that moment, three beautiful women entered the boutique. Sheeka scurried off to the bathroom to clean herself up, and Samara went to go assist the women. Little did Samara know, these three women were going to surprise her.

Chapter Eleven

Ondrej had been sitting in one of his trap houses that sat in the middle of 4th Ave., in between Congress Street and Crane Street, with confusion etched on his face. His decision to kill Leon was biting him in the ass big time. It had been a little close to nine months since Ondrej had shot Leon, and once again his money was coming up missing. At the time, Ondrej thought that taking out Leon was the best option for his operation, only for him to turn around and have this shit happen to him again. Fifteen thousand wasn't what Ondrej called a huge loss compared to the millions that sat in quite a few of his accounts. His OG—Shine—taught him to get an education while he was grinding. Shine told him that it would pay off in the long run, and Ondrej going to Automotive school allowed him to be able to open a few lucrative car shops across the capital region.

"Yo, Dre, my boy!" Richie's voice rang out as the sound of the front door being closed echoed across the room.

"I'm in the kitchen," Ondrej responded. He was increasingly growing tired of this lifestyle day by day. He longed to settle down and enjoy being a husband and a father. Being with Samara had taught him to see himself in that light. At thirty-seven, thirty-eight in a few weeks, he felt like it was his time to exit the game.

Richie stepped into the kitchen dressed in slim-cut ripped Balmain jeans, white and black Balmain cotton sweatshirt with the white Balmain logo on the front, and on his feet were a pair of neoprene and suede black leather low top Balmain sneakers. His black and white Balmain logo baseball cap sat on top of his freshly done cornrows. Richie was a ginger, and females loved that aspect of him to go along with the hood side.

"What's good with you?" Richie asked after taking a seat. He looked at his friend with genuine concern. It's been a long time since he'd seen Ondrej down, and he only hoped that Ondrej wasn't about to deliver bad news.

"Man, it's just some inner turmoil. I'm gonna talk to you about that at another time. I brought you down here because I think I made a fucked up mistake." Ondrej spoke calmly. He lit his blunt and took a massive hit before he passed it to Richie.

"I need you to be more elaborate at what you are trying to tell me."

Ondrej eyed Richie and said, "Leon ain't the one who was stealing from me."

Not for one second did Ondrej think that Richie wasn't taking from him, but he did think that Richie might have known who it was and was protecting them. Richie was a hard book to read, but he had a gentle heart. From what Ondrej did peep, there was no deceit written on Richie's face.

"There's money missing again?" Richie asked, sighing and dropping his head.

"I killed my man for no goddamn reason! Where the fuck is that bitch Destiny at? Why the fuck would she set Leon up for? Do you know who the fuck is taking from me, Richie?"

"Whoa! Whoa! Slow down. Do you really think that I would hide that I knew who was taking it from us? Let me find Destiny and see what she knows or if her story is going to change. In the meantime, cool out. We're gonna figure this shit out. How much is missing?"

"Fifteen thousand."

"So that means that we could probably figure out who's doing it since it's a low amount that was taken. If I hear anything, I'll keep you updated. Matter of fact, I'ma roll out now. Go lay up with wifey and wait for my call." Richie handed the blunt back to Ondrej.

"One more thing."

"What's up?"

"This drop is my last drop. I'm tapping out and will announce my retirement at my birthday dinner. I've slowly been taking precautions with my exit for the past year and a half."

"Here it was, I was thinking you were about to tell me you were leaving the game for a bitch. A bitch you just met no less." Richie chuckled.

"Hol' up, Richie. We've been together for quite a few months but she is still my lady and you're gonna have to respect her as if

132

Unbreak my Heart

we've been together for twenty years. This was taking place before I met her but I'm man enough to admit this woman has made me see things in myself that I never thought I would see. I want things that I know I won't be able to enjoy if I am still in the game."

Richie thought about what Ondrej was saying. Richie had a feeling that Samara would eventually become a problem for their friendship.

"We'll talk about it more when I get some answers. But before I go, I'm going to support your decision no matter what. You're my brother and I want nothing but the best for you. Go home and call it a day."

Ondrej appreciated Richie's words. He needed to hear that. He wasn't so certain that retirement from the game that made him a millionaire was such a good idea. Leaving the house, he was sure as shit that he would be retiring. He would have the time to find his sisters finally, and hopefully make Samara his wife. Ondrej climbed into his car with his thoughts swirling. He hadn't been sure he was coming, and he realized that he could have at least stopped to grab some grocery store flowers. *Fuck it,* he thought as he climbed from his car and made his way up to the front of the door.

"Who is it?" Samara questioned from the opposite side of the door.

"Your man," Ondrej replied cockily, while licking his lips. He patiently waited a few moments before the door swung open and revealed Samara. Instantly, his eyes roamed her body, drinking in every inch of her. Samara was out of her work clothes and was dressed in purple high-waisted Nike biker shorts with a short-sleeved white crop top. Her bubble pink toes called out to Ondrej, and just from a thought of their last session, they had made him constantly brick up.

"You good?" Samara asked, snapping her fingers in front of his face to get his attention. Ondrej walked through the door and folded his body into Samara, wrapping his arms around her.

"I am now. How was work?" Ondrej replied while they walked deeper into the living room.

133

"Work was work. I think it's about time to hire more people. I had a few Karens in the store and needless to say, I almost allowed them enough energy to lose everything I worked so hard for." Samara told Ondrej the story about what happened, and he could do nothing but laugh. By the time she was finished, both of them were on the floor, holding their stomachs laughing.

"Bae, if you would have told me, I would have sent one of my little homie's shorties to handle that," Dre said.

"Shit, they call twelve on black folks all the time when it's a non-emergency. I had to show them they weren't exempt from the shit. The cops being black worked in my favor, and one of them had the nerve to chuckle and call me petty as they were leaving. I'm sick of white people thinking that them being racist is gonna be okay. They're lucky I ain't shoot they ass."

"Stop, you ain't about that life."

Samara turned her head and her face was serious. She replied, "Don't let the designer pantsuits and girly shit fool you. I'm not afraid to shoot a motherfucker if I have to."

"I hear that hot shit," Ondrej said, storing that tidbit of information in the back of his mind. It would be his reminder not to piss Samara off.

"Are you hungry? It's too late to take something out but we can order off of Uber Eats."

"Nah. What I want to eat ain't there." Ondrej was staring at Samara who was trying to refrain from fanning herself. Samara could melt just from him looking at her, and in that moment she was oozing her juices between her legs. Ondrej licked his lips and sprang into action. Since they were already on the floor, he had Samara bend her knees and plant her feet to the floor. His eyes locked with hers as he pulled at her shorts to get them off. Samara's nipples were so hard, she just knew that at any moment they would rip holes in her shirt. As Ondrej slid her shorts and lace boy shorts, he placed wet kisses on different parts of her legs, starting at her calves. The way he caressed her skin while kissing her caused hairs to raise up.

Samara's eyes rolled to the back of her head when she felt Ondrej's tongue against her thighs. She fought the urge to grab his head to place his mouth on her pussy. She enjoyed him taking his time. She used her own hands against her stomach, gripping the bottom of her shirt, which she lifted over her breasts, exposing that she didn't have on a bra. She squeezed and licked her nipples, giving Ondrej a show. Her eyes were closed but under the bright lights Ondrej couldn't take his eyes off of the show. He stopped momentarily to take his shirt off, and Samara's right hand slid from her breasts across her stomach, over her fupa, with her fingers finding her hot spot. Her pussy was sopping wet as she swirled her fingers in her juices on her clit. Ondrej's dick couldn't take the barrier, and he rushed to take his briefs off.

His dick felt heavy in his hand as he used his free hand to coat her juices on it before he slowly stroked himself. After watching Samara pleasure herself for five minutes, she finally was cumming all over her fingers.

"Move your hand," Ondrej demanded as he tapped her hand. She did exactly that and proceeded to watch Ondrej search through his jeans for a condom. His eyebrows snapped together when he came up empty-handed. He grabbed the condom from his drawer when he left the house during the day but he must have left it in the car.

"What happened?" Samara asked.

"I think I left the condom in the car," he replied and looked down at himself. His dick was hard as a boulder.

"It's okay," Samara whispered. She continued, "I'm on birth control and I trust that you haven't been with anyone else being that we have been together almost every day for months."

It only took Ondrej two seconds to make his decision. He wasn't passing up feeling her pussy wrapped around his dick without a condom. Ondrej had come across some good pussy throughout his years, but there was just something about her pussy that fit his rod like a glove. It was always so tight and super wet. There had been plenty of times where after they were done, he pulled away from her with his stomach, pelvis, and thighs all coated with her nectar.

Ondrej laid on his stomach and slid his index finger in between her slit, leaving small circles on her clit. Samara bit down her lip as she moaned. Ondrej replaced his fingers with his tongue, lapping up all of her stickiness. Samara was his favorite meal; she tasted sweet with just a hint of tang. The kind of tang that a pussy is supposed to have. Minutes later, Samara was holding his head in place while she grinded her pussy on his tongue. Her legs shook and her toes curled once she felt the release of her orgasm splash onto his mouth, tongue, and face.

"Damn, you taste good." Ondrej moaned against Samara's pussy. Ondrej sat up on his knees as his face glistened with her sweet juices. He looked at Samara who was panting, trying to regain her composure. Ondrej grabbed his tool and placed his head in her opening. Samara arched her back while Ondrej slowly entered her, savoring the tightness. *Oh, I'm about to tear this little pussy up for sure!* Ondrej thought to himself. He was in heaven as he slowly moved in and out of her. His head dropped to the crook of her neck as he softly bit her and placed kisses on her. Samara's body shook like an earthquake as her body deceived her and she came back to back all over his dick.

"You like when I stroke you like this?" Ondrej asked. His body was close to hers, and he was in a planking position with her legs spread-eagle, while slowly moving around in her gushy pussy. He never experienced macaroni-sounding pussy, but that's what it sounded exactly like between her legs.

"Oh my God, yes!" Samara moaned as her hands roamed around his back, trying not to dig her nails deep into his skin. Ondrej smirked. He was far from cocky but when it came to his pipe game, he knew for sure that his shit was up to par and knew what danger his weapon held. Ondrej pulled out of Samara, and had her flip over and toot her ass up in the air. Dre positioned himself on his knees and gripped Samara by the waist.

"Yeah, bae! Throw that ass back and cum all over this dick again." Ondrej gritted through his teeth. Ondrej tore Samara's ass up and by the time they were done, they both were breathing heavily, mouths dry, clothes everywhere, and silent. Ondrej went back to thinking about his retirement. Everything in him wanted to retire but there was an unsettling feeling inside of him that kept gnawing at him.

"Bae, you good?" Samara asked. Ondrej was so wrapped up in his thoughts that he didn't notice Samara get up and went to get a wet rag.

"Yeah, I'm straight. I just got a few things on my mind." He responded and reached for the rag. She swatted his hand away and squatted in between his legs to clean him off.

"I'm gonna make some popcorn and a few other snacks. It's still kind of early. You want to pig out and watch movies?" Samara asked. Never in his adult life had he had a woman clean him off. He was the one doing the clean-up.

"I'm down."

"Are you sure you good?"

Ondrej chuckled and said, "I'm sure. I'm just a little speechless at the moment. I don't know if I should thank you or tell you to unhand me."

Samara didn't realize what she was doing. After she and Ryan would finish, he liked for her to clean him off. She's had plenty of sex with Ondrej, but this was the first time she did this. She laughed deep from her belly and took this situation as a sign that she was comfortable enough to let her guard down. When she was done cleaning him, she went into the laundry room to place the rag with the clothes she was putting in the wash the next day. When she came back, Ondrej was pulling up his briefs.

"You ready?" Samara asked. She had lust written in her eyes, and he wasn't sure if Samara was talking about the movie or another round.

He asked just that, "Round two or the movie?"

Samara eyed him from head to toe while drawing her bottom lip in between her teeth. She smirked and said, "Round two." And with that she ran off in a fit of giggles while Ondrej gave chase. Rounds two, three, and four popped off and they never got to watch their movie.

Mimi

Chapter Twelve

Three Weeks Later (July 26th)

"Can you please sit your ass down so we can get started on your make-up?" Sheeka sighed. Ondrej's thirty-eighth birthday dinner was set to begin in just four hours at eight o' clock. Samara had been so grateful that Ondrej suggested that she hire an event planner for the dinner. She didn't know how she would have pulled it off had she done it herself. Mia was the best event planner in the Capital District, and her work spoke for itself. All Samara had to do was give Mia a general idea of what she wanted and her color scheme, and like magic she came up with the most beautiful set-up she had ever seen. Samara wanted to make sure that Ondrej enjoyed himself to the fullest extent, so she opted on the color theme being his favorite color. Ondrej's favorite color was brown, and Samara wouldn't have been able to deal with the stress that it came with to find decorations that matched with brown. But Mia did the damn thing without much effort. She was truly gifted.

Before Samara and her girls were to get glammed up, Samara had the pleasure of seeing what the finishing product looked like. She was in awe at all of the browns, nudes, creams, and beiges Mia had pulled up. Samara had booked the Terrace at Water's Edge, and the dining hall was magnificent. There was a wooden dance floor in the center of the room with six tables that seated five around the dance floor. Dimly lit gold and crystal chandeliers hung from the ceilings as if they were scattered rain drops. On the back wall was a black ceiling-to-floor backdrop with two white six feet tall throne chairs that were trimmed in gold in front. Those chairs were reserved for Samara and Ondrej. Their circle glass top table sat in front of the chairs covered in a brown table cloth, with accents of cream, gold, and white. Each table looked the same, and the only difference between Ondrej's and Samara's table from the others was that the guest tables had three different sized square glasses that held pebbles, water, a white rose, and a floating tea candle. Ondrej and Samara's table held a sixteen-inch, five-arm crystal chandelier candle holder. The room was semi-dimly lit and had a relaxing feel to it.

"I can't sit down, Sheeka. I'm nervous." Samara pouted as she squeezed one hand inside of the other.

"It's a birthday dinner, not your wedding day. Chill out." Samirah spoke through clenched teeth. She was getting her make-up done, and the make-up artist was applying lipstick.

"I haven't told anyone this, but I got a surprise for Ondrej. But he also said that he had an announcement to make, and it's making my stomach feel like a thousand knots are twisting tighter and tighter."

"What's the surprise?" Amber asked. Sheeka looked up from what she was doing and looked to Samara. She was the only one who knew about the surprise, and she was shocked that Samara didn't tell Amber or her sister.

"I don't want to say. At least not right now, but I know for a fact that he's gonna love it," Samara stated.

"Chile, you are raising my blood pressure. If you are confident that he's gonna love it, then there is no reason for you to be nervous. Take a shot and calm your ass down!" Samirah said. Samara knew her sister was right, but it didn't change the knots in her stomach. Samara nodded. She was tripping over the fact that she was this nervous. Taking Amber's advice, she walked over to the table where she took a shot of Patron. She was about to take her seat again and decided to take another shot. She needed it.

"Okay, come on, Sheeka. Let's get this shit started."

The day before, Samara had gotten her hair done and was rocking a thirty-inch Brazilian straight sew-in with a side part. Sheeka slayed her friend's face in a natural look and moved onto Amber. Sheeka knew that Samirah was being petty by hiring her own make-up artist, but Sheeka wasn't moved by it. She still fucked with Samirah the long way but if she kept being petty towards her for whatever reason, then she would see to it that she would find out her answers. When it was time for them to get dressed, they all were feeling tipsy and what nerves Samara had were now non-existent. They were playing music, dancing, and enjoying themselves. At seven-thirty, Samara went to her bedroom and began to get dressed. For the dinner, she chose to rock a Herve Leger's cream bodycon dress that had a sheer overlay, crisscross straps at the back, and a bustier inspired bodice. It hugged every curve of her just right. Not to mention that her ass looked perfect, and her girls sat high and beautiful. On her feet she was wearing YSL Casandra sandals with the black monogram.

"You just starting to get dressed?" Samara's body stiffened, and chills—good ones—ran down her spine at the sound of Ondrej's voice. He caught her with her ass in the air as she was grabbing her shoe box from the floor of the closet.

"Me and the girls lost track of time," Samara replied and almost melted when she turned attention to Ondrej. He was wearing a cream colored three-piece suit, a white button-up, and a brown bow tie. On his feet were a pair of apron tow Alexander Mcqueen brown penny loafers. His Hermes cologne intoxicated her, but most importantly it was him cutting his hair that knocked her socks off. Her mouth dropped open and as much as he didn't want to, Ondrej blushed and a smirk appeared on his face.

"You cut your fucking hair!" Samara stated in shock. She wanted to tell him he looked fucking delectable, but she was just in shock that he cut his hair.

Ondrej rubbed his hand against the top of his head and asked, "You don't like it?"

"Samara walked up to him and held his gaze and she said, "I'm a little shocked but I love it. You no longer have a baby face and you actually look like you're in your late twenties, early thirties."

"You got a nigga blushing and shit. But I'm gonna need you to hurry up and get dressed so we can go." Ondrej moved closer to Samara, placed one hand on her ass and his other on her chin to raise her lips to his.

"Mmm—yes, sir," Samara replied after a few seconds. She knew that if she didn't break the kiss, they would arrive at dinner late. Samara turned away from him and dropped her robe. Within seconds, Ondrej's dick pumped with blood as he watched Samara being petty and bend over at the waist to grab her shoes. Ondrej cleared the distance between them, wrapped his left hand softly around her throat, and his right hand on her stomach, pulling her close.

Ondrej whispered in her ear. "Hurry up and get dressed, not gonna play into your games right now because you know how I hate to be late for things. Hurry up before I put this dick up in you." He left a wet trail of kisses on her neck and left the room. Samara had to take a moment to fan herself. Her kitty was moist and she cursed herself. Ondrej grabbed onto her neck, applying just enough for her to feel and not hurt her, setting a fire off in her.

"Let me get my ass dressed," Samara said out loud. Shaking her head, she slid into her dress, placed her shoes on her feet and took her bonnet off to comb out her hair. Silver bangles adorned her wrists, diamond studs in her ears. She sprayed on a little bit of *Pour Femme* by Versace, and made her entrance downstairs.

"About time, bitch," Samirah said once she saw her baby sister enter the living room. Her sister looked phenomenal, and she immediately took out her phone and began snapping pictures which led to them flicking it up with Sheeka, Amber, and Ondrej. He wasn't for pictures but he figured that he would hop in a few with Samara in the spirit of keeping the rest of the night positive.

They arrived at the Terrace just shy of eight-forty-five, and were greeted with applause. The guests that were invited were all of the people that Ondrej trusted and had genuine love from. Ondrej, being the star of the show, made his rounds with dapping people up while Samara made her rounds with making sure that everybody was satisfied. The liquor was flowing freely due to the open bar, and the music pumped throughout the speakers as if they were in a club.

Richie walked into the hall a half an hour after Ondrej and Samara did. He too wore a cream colored suit, and his hair was freshly braided. He wore his grills in his mouth, and the women in the room who already wasn't with a dude were falling at his feet. Samara eyed Richie from across the room with disgust written on her face.

"Sis, fix your face," Amber scolded under her breath.

Unbreak my Heart

"I don't like that nigga," Samara responded as she watched Richie and Ondrej exchange daps. Ondrej peered behind Richie, and his face changed at something behind him. Samara noticed this and looked where Ondrej was looking, and there was that bitch Destiny, that she knew for sure that she didn't invite. She left Amber where she was standing and made her way to her man.

"Richie, let me holla at you for a quick second," Ondrej was saying when Samara approached him. His jaw was tense, and Samara knew he was tight. She looked at Destiny who stood with a smirk on her face. Ondrej walked off, and Richie went after him.

"What's good?" Richie asked when they were away from Samara and Destiny.

"Something about that woman screams snake and you continue to bring her around. Leon didn't even bring her around as much as you do. Is there something between y'all that you want to tell me about?"

"Did you or did you not ask me to get close to the bitch to find out what she knows?"

"My nigga, it's been three weeks, you ain't find shit out but you bring her to my birthday dinner, knowing my lady was gonna be here and she don't like her."

"With all due respect, Dre, I don't know shorty and I could care less about who she likes and who she doesn't like. Because my best man asked me to do something, but it seems to be a problem."

Ondrej sighed because Richie wasn't hearing him. He said with finality, "I want the bitch gone. I don't give a fuck what you got to do but the hoe got to go."

Ondrej tapped Richie in the chest twice as he walked away to go join his lady who he could tell was about to blow her top. Richie felt like he was sonned, and it wasn't sitting right with him. Ondrej was his man but Richie had been feeling more like a worker than the boss that he was. Maybe he was overthinking things but as soon as the dinner was over, Richie knew that he was gonna have to chop it up with his boys.

"Do you know who I am? Nah, I don't think that you do because if you did, you would know how to speak to me!" Destiny loudly spoke, causing some people to turn in their direction.

"Bitch, obviously I don't give a fuck who you are. I said what the fuck I said and I stand ten toes on that. I just know you better take heed and move the fuck around because, bitch, this ain't nothing that you want to play with," Samara calmly replied as she started to come out of her heels. Sheeka, Amber, and Samirah saw the exchange, and stopped what they were doing and headed on over.

"Bae, put your shoes back on," Ondrej said, standing in between Samara and Destiny so that her focus was diverted to him. The last thing that he wanted was a fight to break out. He just wanted one night of peace and fun.

"Nah, 'cause this hoe thinks she is something when she ain't about nothing, and I'm ready to dog walk her ass around this room. Move out of my way, Ondrej."

"Yo, Richie, handle that!" Ondrej seethed. Richie walked over to them and grabbed Destiny by the elbow and dragged her toward the exit.

"Sis, you good?" Sheeka asked.

"She's always good when she around me," Ondrej replied. His eyes were on Samara, letting her know that he would always be her protector when he was around.

"I'm good, y'all. Let's get back to what we came to do." Samara ran her fingers through her hair and placed her shoe back on her foot. Ondrej needed to have a talk with Richie. Something was brewing, and his gut only confirmed it.

The drama that had only slightly unfolded was pushed to the back of everybody's minds as they began to drink again and get on the dance floor. Food was being served buffet style, and the guests had free reign on when they wanted to eat. Around eleven o'clock Samara was ready to reveal her surprise to Ondrej. She looked around the room, making sure that everyone was accounted for. Walking over to the DJ booth, Samara asked the DJ for the microphone and asked him to cut the music. Everybody in the room turned their attention to the DJ, and he threw up his hands in mock surrender. Samara shook her head and laughed.

"How's everyone feeling tonight?" Samara asked into the microphone, causing people to cheer. She continued: "As everyone knows, tonight is a very special night for a very special man. I haven't had the pleasure of knowing him for as long as everyone here, but the time that I have gotten to know him has been the best. He was the sunshine when I was in a dark spot and I can't be more thankful."

Meanwhile—

Richie stared down at Destiny who was pacing back and forth fuming. She was mumbling under her breath about how Richie was a bitch when it came to Ondrej. Richie looked on nonchalantly because at this point he was disappointed in falling for this woman. He knew it was wrong because Leon was his boy just as much as he was Ondrej's. He should have known that she had some shit with her when she told him that she wanted Leon out of the picture. Richie came up with the plan to lie on Leon and say that he was taking from Ondrej. Richie was Ondrej's brother in some sense, and he knew that Ondrej would take his word over Leon's. Richie falling in love with Destiny wasn't in the plans, but they had gotten closer since Leon was murdered, and he was now smacking himself in the forehead for doing so.

"You just let that nigga and his bitch just speak to me any kind of way. And why you ain't telling nobody about us. You said that you loved me, Richie!" Destiny fumed.

"Yo, you need to chill the fuck out. You acting like that ain't my brother out there. I don't like his bitch neither but what can I fucking do?"

Destiny snorted and looked at him. "That's your brother but before you found out that he was retiring, you wanted to kill the nigga for his spot. Tuh! You portray that you are loyal to him and I get the short end of the stick. But in actuality, for the past year and a half, I've been more loyal to you more than anything. You can't even

145

announce that we together because you afraid of what that nigga might find out."

"You need to chill out with all that rah rah shit. Just go home, Destiny, and I'll be there and we can discuss this after the party." Richie was tired of hearing her bump her gums. That's all she did, and he was very tired of it. *Why can't women be good with what the situation is without a title?* Richie thought to himself. He headed back toward the direction of the hall as Destiny stared daggers into his back.

"Oh, you just wait and see. You are not about making moves, we'll see about that. I got something for everybody." Destiny fumed and marched off to the nearest exit. She wasn't going home, but she was for damn sure about to test every gangsta that was in that room.

Back at the Party—

"Happpppyyyy Birthdayyyyyy, dear Ondrejjjjjjjjjj! Happy Birthday to youuuuuuu!" The crowd sang as a server came out of the kitchen rolling a four-tiered red velvet cake that was covered in black fondant and on the sides of each tier was a stencil of his younger self and his sisters. The cake almost brought a tear to his eye as he examined the faces of his sisters. He mumbled an apology to the pictures because every day he battled with himself for letting them down and not being able to find them. Samara watched him as he looked at the pictures and tears ran down her face, ruining her make-up.

"Before we cut the cake, I have a surprise for you," Samara announced into the mic.

Ondrej eyed Samara and pulled her off to the side and said, "Shorty, if you about to tell me that you carrying my seed, this ain't the place for that. Wait till we get home."

"Nigga, I'm not pregnant. You know like hell I'm on birth control, now move."

Nerves built up in Samara but she shook it off and placed the mic back to her mouth. She said, "Ladies."

Three women stood up and Ondrej looked on in confusion. He knew damn well Samara didn't hire no damn strippers for his party.

146

He could see strippers any day of the week, and he was curious as to why she would get him strippers. He then noticed the excitement on the women's faces and how they all looked familiar, but he couldn't pinpoint where he knew them from.

"A while ago when I had that situation happen at my boutique, these three lovely women walked in. I greeted them as usual and told them if they needed any help to let me know. I was amazed at how beautiful they were and told my friend Sheeka so that day. They were talking amongst themselves and when they started calling each other by their names, I just knew that I hit the jackpot. Bae, these three women are your sisters! Damani, Kamani, and Ishani!"

The tears that collected in his sockets blinded him but he wouldn't be able to live in this rejoice for much longer. Time seemed to move slowly at the realization, and he saw his sisters making their way over to him.

Blocka! Blocka! Blocka!

Pop! Pop! Pop!

Gunfire erupted, and everyone's instinct was to get low to the ground. The seconds that it took for everyone to realize what was going on, the damage had been done already. The gangstas in the room returned fire but it was no use. They were caught off guard, and quite a few people were killed as casualties. The room was in pandemonium while Richie fired back. His eyes were sweeping the room, trying to find his partner but didn't see him with any luck. At the exit, a figure stood in the door, holding a flame to the tip of the blunt. Taking a toke of the blunt, the thick cloud of smoke served as a cover for them to disappear. Richie's anger boiled in his chest as he ran after the figure. There was about to be mayhem and bloodshed.

"Noooooooooooo! Call 911! My baby has been shot!" Samara yelled through the chaos. It was like she was chanting it as she balanced herself on her knees, holding her hands against Dre's stomach to slow the bleeding. Dre's eyes fluttered as he listened in oblivion. The gunfire had stopped. Thankfully, he heard sirens in the distance. He opened his eyes slightly and saw the face of his shorty. All he could think about was placing the ring on her finger, which was in his pocket. Now he knew that he would never get the chance to do that.

To Be Continued…
Unbreak my Heart 2
Coming Soon

Unbreak my Heart

Lock Down Publications and Ca$h Presents assisted publishing packages.

BASIC PACKAGE $499

Editing

Cover Design

Formatting

UPGRADED PACKAGE $800

Typing

Editing

Cover Design

Formatting

ADVANCE PACKAGE $1,200

Typing

Editing

Cover Design

Formatting

Copyright registration

Proofreading

Upload book to Amazon

Mimi

LDP SUPREME PACKAGE $1,500

Typing

Editing

Cover Design

Formatting

Copyright registration

Proofreading

Set up Amazon account

Upload book to Amazon

Advertise on LDP Amazon and Facebook page

***Other services available upon request. Additional charges may apply

Lock Down Publications

P.O. Box 944

Stockbridge, GA 30281-9998

Phone # 470 303-9761

Submission Guideline

Submit the first three chapters of your completed manuscript to ldpsubmissions@gmail.com, subject line: Your book's title. The manuscript must be in a .doc file and sent as an attachment. Document should be in Times New Roman, double spaced and in size 12 font. Also, provide your synopsis and full contact information. If sending multiple submissions, they must each be in a separate email.

Have a story but no way to send it electronically? You can still submit to LDP/Ca$h Presents. Send in the first three chapters, written or typed, of your completed manuscript to:

LDP: Submissions Dept
Po Box 944
Stockbridge, Ga 30281

DO NOT send original manuscript. Must be a duplicate.

Provide your synopsis and a cover letter containing your full contact information.

Thanks for considering LDP and Ca$h Presents.

<u>NEW RELEASES</u>

BORN IN THE GRAVE by SELF MADE TAY

MOAN IN MY MOUTH by XTASY

SKI MASK MONEY by RENTA

C.R.E.A.M. 3 by YOLANDA MOORE

UNBREAK MY HEART by MIMI

Unbreak my Heart

Mimi

STRAIGHT BEAST MODE III

De'Kari

KINGPIN KILLAZ IV

STREET KINGS III

PAID IN BLOOD III

CARTEL KILLAZ IV

DOPE GODS III

Hood Rich

SINS OF A HUSTLA II

ASAD

RICH $AVAGE II

By Martell Troublesome Bolden

YAYO V

Bred In The Game 2

S. Allen

THE STREETS WILL TALK II

By Yolanda Moore

SON OF A DOPE FIEND III

HEAVEN GOT A GHETTO II

SKI MASK MONEY II

By Renta

LOYALTY AIN'T PROMISED III

By Keith Williams

I'M NOTHING WITHOUT HIS LOVE II

SINS OF A THUG II

TO THE THUG I LOVED BEFORE II

IN A HUSTLER I TRUST II

By Monet Dragun

QUIET MONEY IV

EXTENDED CLIP III

Unbreak my Heart

THUG LIFE IV

By **Trai'Quan**

THE STREETS MADE ME IV

By **Larry D. Wright**

IF YOU CROSS ME ONCE II

ANGEL IV

By **Anthony Fields**

THE STREETS WILL NEVER CLOSE IV

By **K'ajji**

HARD AND RUTHLESS III

KILLA KOUNTY III

By **Khufu**

MONEY GAME III

By **Smoove Dolla**

JACK BOYS VS DOPE BOYS II

A GANGSTA'S QUR'AN V

COKE GIRLZ II

COKE BOYS II

By **Romell Tukes**

MURDA WAS THE CASE II

Elijah R. Freeman

THE STREETS NEVER LET GO II

By **Robert Baptiste**

AN UNFORESEEN LOVE IV

By **Meesha**

KING OF THE TRENCHES III

by **GHOST & TRANAY ADAMS**

MONEY MAFIA II

By **Jibril Williams**

Mimi

QUEEN OF THE ZOO III
By **Black Migo**
VICIOUS LOYALTY III
By Kingpen
A GANGSTA'S PAIN III
By J-Blunt
CONFESSIONS OF A JACKBOY III
By Nicholas Lock
GRIMEY WAYS III
By Ray Vinci
KING KILLA II
By Vincent "Vitto" Holloway
BETRAYAL OF A THUG II
By Fre$h
THE MURDER QUEENS II
By Michael Gallon
THE BIRTH OF A GANGSTER III
By Delmont Player
TREAL LOVE II
By Le'Monica Jackson
FOR THE LOVE OF BLOOD II
By Jamel Mitchell
RAN OFF ON DA PLUG II
By Paper Boi Rari
HOOD CONSIGLIERE II
By Keese
PRETTY GIRLS DO NASTY THINGS II
By Nicole Goosby
PROTÉGÉ OF A LEGEND II
By Corey Robinson

Unbreak my Heart

IT'S JUST ME AND YOU II
By Ah'Million
BORN IN THE GRAVE II
By Self Made Tay

Available Now

RESTRAINING ORDER **I & II**
By **CA$H & Coffee**
LOVE KNOWS NO BOUNDARIES **I II & III**
By **Coffee**
RAISED AS A GOON I, II, III & IV
BRED BY THE SLUMS I, II, III
BLAST FOR ME I & II
ROTTEN TO THE CORE I II III
A BRONX TALE I, II, III
DUFFLE BAG CARTEL I II III IV V VI
HEARTLESS GOON I II III IV V
A SAVAGE DOPEBOY I II
DRUG LORDS I II III
CUTTHROAT MAFIA I II
KING OF THE TRENCHES
By **Ghost**
LAY IT DOWN **I & II**
LAST OF A DYING BREED I II
BLOOD STAINS OF A SHOTTA I & II III
By **Jamaica**

Mimi

LOYAL TO THE GAME I II III

LIFE OF SIN I, II III

By **TJ & Jelissa**

BLOODY COMMAS I & II

SKI MASK CARTEL I II & III

KING OF NEW YORK I II,III IV V

RISE TO POWER I II III

COKE KINGS I II III IV V

BORN HEARTLESS I II III IV

KING OF THE TRAP I II

By **T.J. Edwards**

IF LOVING HIM IS WRONG…I & II

LOVE ME EVEN WHEN IT HURTS I II III

By **Jelissa**

WHEN THE STREETS CLAP BACK I & II III

THE HEART OF A SAVAGE I II III IV

MONEY MAFIA

LOYAL TO THE SOIL I II III

By **Jibril Williams**

A DISTINGUISHED THUG STOLE MY HEART I II & III

LOVE SHOULDN'T HURT I II III IV

RENEGADE BOYS I II III IV

PAID IN KARMA I II III

SAVAGE STORMS I II III

AN UNFORESEEN LOVE I II III

By **Meesha**

A GANGSTER'S CODE I &, II III

A GANGSTER'S SYN I II III

THE SAVAGE LIFE I II III

CHAINED TO THE STREETS I II III

Unbreak my Heart

BLOOD ON THE MONEY I II III

A GANGSTA'S PAIN I II

By J-Blunt

PUSH IT TO THE LIMIT

By **Bre' Hayes**

BLOOD OF A BOSS **I, II, III, IV, V**

SHADOWS OF THE GAME

TRAP BASTARD

By **Askari**

THE STREETS BLEED MURDER **I, II & III**

THE HEART OF A GANGSTA I II& III

By **Jerry Jackson**

CUM FOR ME I II III IV V VI VII VIII

An **LDP Erotica Collaboration**

BRIDE OF A HUSTLA **I II & II**

THE FETTI GIRLS **I, II& III**

CORRUPTED BY A GANGSTA I, II III, IV

BLINDED BY HIS LOVE

THE PRICE YOU PAY FOR LOVE I, II ,III

DOPE GIRL MAGIC I II III

By **Destiny Skai**

WHEN A GOOD GIRL GOES BAD

By **Adrienne**

THE COST OF LOYALTY I II III

By Kweli

A GANGSTER'S REVENGE **I II III & IV**

THE BOSS MAN'S DAUGHTERS I II III IV V

A SAVAGE LOVE **I & II**

BAE BELONGS TO ME I II

A HUSTLER'S DECEIT I, II, III

Mimi

WHAT BAD BITCHES DO I, II, III
SOUL OF A MONSTER I II III
KILL ZONE
A DOPE BOY'S QUEEN I II III
TIL DEATH
By **Aryanna**
A KINGPIN'S AMBITON
A KINGPIN'S AMBITION **II**
I MURDER FOR THE DOUGH
By **Ambitious**
TRUE SAVAGE I II III IV V VI VII
DOPE BOY MAGIC I, II, III
MIDNIGHT CARTEL I II III
CITY OF KINGZ I II
NIGHTMARE ON SILENT AVE
THE PLUG OF LIL MEXICO II
CLASSIC CITY
By **Chris Green**
A DOPEBOY'S PRAYER
By **Eddie "Wolf" Lee**
THE KING CARTEL **I, II & III**
By **Frank Gresham**
THESE NIGGAS AIN'T LOYAL **I, II & III**
By **Nikki Tee**
GANGSTA SHYT **I II &III**
By **CATO**
THE ULTIMATE BETRAYAL
By **Phoenix**
BOSS'N UP **I , II & III**
By **Royal Nicole**

160

Unbreak my Heart

I LOVE YOU TO DEATH
By **Destiny J**
I RIDE FOR MY HITTA
I STILL RIDE FOR MY HITTA
By **Misty Holt**
LOVE & CHASIN' PAPER
By **Qay Crockett**
TO DIE IN VAIN
SINS OF A HUSTLA
By **ASAD**
BROOKLYN HUSTLAZ
By **Boogsy Morina**
BROOKLYN ON LOCK I & II
By **Sonovia**
GANGSTA CITY
By **Teddy Duke**
A DRUG KING AND HIS DIAMOND I & II III
A DOPEMAN'S RICHES
HER MAN, MINE'S TOO I, II
CASH MONEY HO'S
THE WIFEY I USED TO BE I II
PRETTY GIRLS DO NASTY THINGS
By Nicole Goosby
TRAPHOUSE KING **I II & III**
KINGPIN KILLAZ I II III
STREET KINGS I II
PAID IN BLOOD **I II**
CARTEL KILLAZ I II III
DOPE GODS I II
By **Hood Rich**

Mimi

LIPSTICK KILLAH **I, II, III**

CRIME OF PASSION I II & III

FRIEND OR FOE I II III

By **Mimi**

STEADY MOBBN' **I, II, III**

THE STREETS STAINED MY SOUL I II III

By **Marcellus Allen**

WHO SHOT YA **I, II, III**

SON OF A DOPE FIEND I II

HEAVEN GOT A GHETTO

SKI MASK MONEY

Renta

GORILLAZ IN THE BAY **I II III IV**

TEARS OF A GANGSTA I II

3X KRAZY I II

STRAIGHT BEAST MODE I II

DE'KARI

TRIGGADALE I II III

MURDAROBER WAS THE CASE

Elijah R. Freeman

GOD BLESS THE TRAPPERS I, II, III

THESE SCANDALOUS STREETS I, II, III

FEAR MY GANGSTA I, II, III IV, V

THESE STREETS DON'T LOVE NOBODY I, II

BURY ME A G I, II, III, IV, V

A GANGSTA'S EMPIRE I, II, III, IV

THE DOPEMAN'S BODYGAURD I II

THE REALEST KILLAZ I II III

THE LAST OF THE OGS I II III

Tranay Adams

Unbreak my Heart

THE STREETS ARE CALLING

Duquie Wilson

MARRIED TO A BOSS I II III

By Destiny Skai & Chris Green

KINGZ OF THE GAME I II III IV V VI

Playa Ray

SLAUGHTER GANG I II III

RUTHLESS HEART I II III

By Willie Slaughter

FUK SHYT

By Blakk Diamond

DON'T F#CK WITH MY HEART I II

By Linnea

ADDICTED TO THE DRAMA I II III

IN THE ARM OF HIS BOSS II

By Jamila

YAYO I II III IV

A SHOOTER'S AMBITION I II

BRED IN THE GAME

By S. Allen

TRAP GOD I II III

RICH $AVAGE

MONEY IN THE GRAVE I II III

By Martell Troublesome Bolden

FOREVER GANGSTA

GLOCKS ON SATIN SHEETS I II

By Adrian Dulan

TOE TAGZ I II III IV

LEVELS TO THIS SHYT I II

IT'S JUST ME AND YOU

Mimi

By Ah'Million

KINGPIN DREAMS I II III

RAN OFF ON DA PLUG

By Paper Boi Rari

CONFESSIONS OF A GANGSTA I II III IV

CONFESSIONS OF A JACKBOY I II

By Nicholas Lock

I'M NOTHING WITHOUT HIS LOVE

SINS OF A THUG

TO THE THUG I LOVED BEFORE

A GANGSTA SAVED XMAS

IN A HUSTLER I TRUST

By Monet Dragun

CAUGHT UP IN THE LIFE I II III

THE STREETS NEVER LET GO

By Robert Baptiste

NEW TO THE GAME I II III

MONEY, MURDER & MEMORIES I II III

By **Malik D. Rice**

LIFE OF A SAVAGE I II III

A GANGSTA'S QUR'AN I II III IV

MURDA SEASON I II III

GANGLAND CARTEL I II III

CHI'RAQ GANGSTAS I II III

KILLERS ON ELM STREET I II III

JACK BOYZ N DA BRONX I II III

A DOPEBOY'S DREAM I II III

JACK BOYS VS DOPE BOYS

COKE GIRLZ

COKE BOYS

Unbreak my Heart

By Romell Tukes

LOYALTY AIN'T PROMISED I II

By Keith Williams

QUIET MONEY I II III

THUG LIFE I II III

EXTENDED CLIP I II

By **Trai'Quan**

THE STREETS MADE ME I II III

By **Larry D. Wright**

THE ULTIMATE SACRIFICE I, II, III, IV, V, VI

KHADIFI

IF YOU CROSS ME ONCE

ANGEL I II III

IN THE BLINK OF AN EYE

By **Anthony Fields**

THE LIFE OF A HOOD STAR

By Ca$h & Rashia Wilson

THE STREETS WILL NEVER CLOSE I II III

By K'ajji

CREAM I II III

THE STREETS WILL TALK

By Yolanda Moore

NIGHTMARES OF A HUSTLA I II III

By King Dream

CONCRETE KILLA I II III

VICIOUS LOYALTY I II

By Kingpen

HARD AND RUTHLESS I II

MOB TOWN 251

THE BILLIONAIRE BENTLEYS I II III

Mimi

By Von Diesel
GHOST MOB
Stilloan Robinson
MOB TIES I II III IV V VI
By SayNoMore
BODYMORE MURDERLAND I II III
THE BIRTH OF A GANGSTER I II
By Delmont Player
FOR THE LOVE OF A BOSS
By C. D. Blue
MOBBED UP I II III IV
THE BRICK MAN I II III IV
THE COCAINE PRINCESS I II III IV V
By King Rio
KILLA KOUNTY I II III
By Khufu
MONEY GAME I II
By Smoove Dolla
A GANGSTA'S KARMA I II
By FLAME
KING OF THE TRENCHES I II
by **GHOST & TRANAY ADAMS**
QUEEN OF THE ZOO I II
By **Black Migo**
GRIMEY WAYS I II
By Ray Vinci
XMAS WITH AN ATL SHOOTER
By Ca$h & Destiny Skai
KING KILLA
By Vincent "Vitto" Holloway

166

Unbreak my Heart

BETRAYAL OF A THUG
By Fre$h
THE MURDER QUEENS
By Michael Gallon
TREAL LOVE
By Le'Monica Jackson
FOR THE LOVE OF BLOOD
By Jamel Mitchell
HOOD CONSIGLIERE
By Keese
PROTÉGÉ OF A LEGEND
By Corey Robinson
BORN IN THE GRAVE
By Self Made Tay
MOAN IN MY MOUTH
By XTASY

BOOKS BY LDP'S CEO, CA$H

TRUST IN NO MAN

TRUST IN NO MAN 2

TRUST IN NO MAN 3

BONDED BY BLOOD

SHORTY GOT A THUG

THUGS CRY

THUGS CRY 2

THUGS CRY 3

TRUST NO BITCH

TRUST NO BITCH 2

TRUST NO BITCH 3

TIL MY CASKET DROPS

RESTRAINING ORDER

RESTRAINING ORDER 2

IN LOVE WITH A CONVICT

LIFE OF A HOOD STAR

XMAS WITH AN ATL SHOOTER

Unbreak my Heart

Unbreak my Heart

WITHDRAWN

CPSIA information can be obtained
at www.ICGtesting.com
Printed in the USA
LVHW080922250223
740361LV00005B/151